"You have to admit t[...] between us."

"That's not the point," Jane insisted. "Neither of us is suited for a relationship."

"I'm going to play dumb for a second so you can tell me why we're not suited for one another," Holden replied.

"There's no way I could ever bring you home to my family."

"Last time I checked I was a pretty good catch."

"It's nothing to do with you. It's the way my family would perceive you."

"I'm confused. You're saying it's not me, it's your family?"

"Sort of."

"Oh, good. For a second I thought you were throwing up imaginary obstacles," he said. "Listen, just admit that you and I shared something pretty incredible. And I'll leave it at that."

"You'll drop it?"

"Sure," he lied. "Just admit that I rocked your world and we'll go back to being simply partners without benefits."

"Okay, Holden. You were pretty amazing and quite possibly the best guy I've ever slept with. Is that enough?"

"Yeah, it'll do. Now tell me again why we shouldn't be partners with benefits?"

"You're impossible."

Dear Reader,

Go big or go home—that was the prevailing mantra that kept running through my head with the final chapter in this exciting series of books. The stakes are the highest they've ever been, the characters rich with life and the situation without easy answers. Of course, it makes for good reading, but it makes for really hard writing! This book didn't come together easily, but it was worth the trouble, as I think this story is one of the best (which is hard for me to say because all my books are like my babies).

I hope you enjoy *The Agent's Surrender* with its twists and turns and ultimate conclusion. If you're just coming to this story, you might want to check out *The Sniper,* which is Nathan's story, and *Moving Target,* which is Jake's story. Both are a great complement to Jane and Holden's story.

Hearing from readers is a special joy. Please feel free to drop me a line via email through my website at www.kimberlyvanmeter.com or through snail mail at Kimberly Van Meter, P.O. Box 2210, Oakdale, CA 95361.

All the best,

Kimberly

THE AGENT'S SURRENDER

—

Kimberly Van Meter

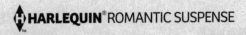

HARLEQUIN® ROMANTIC SUSPENSE

ISBN-13: 978-0-373-27891-6

THE AGENT'S SURRENDER

Copyright © 2014 by Kimberly Sheetz

Printed in U.S.A.

www.Harlequin.com

Books by Kimberly Van Meter

Harlequin Romantic Suspense

Silhouette Romantic Suspense

Harlequin Superromance

Other titles by this author available in ebook format.

KIMBERLY VAN METER

wrote her first book at sixteen and finally achieved publication in December 2006. She writes for the Harlequin Superromance and Harlequin Romantic Suspense lines. She and her husband of seventeen years have three children, three cats and always a houseful of friends, family and fun.

With all my love and admiration...

To my editor, Johanna Raisanen...you've taken my words and made them shine. I'm so lucky to have you on my side. From *The Call* to now, we're a great team, and I am so grateful for your wisdom, your guidance and your talent! Here's to many more collaborative books in our future.

Chapter 1

"They can't do this." Holden Archangelo, CIA special skills officer, held his temper by the thinnest margin as his superior, Reed Harris, chief of staff, military affairs, looked up at Holden's sudden appearance in his office. Holden gripped the door frame with Jane Fallon hot on his heels. "There's been a mistake," he said, ignoring Jane's rigid, unwelcome presence.

"Your personal feelings are clouding your judgment," Jane cut in, her lithe and muscular frame nearly as stiff as her inability to see Holden's side. "If the accused were anyone other than your twin brother, would you have the same objections?"

He ignored her point. "Miko's innocent."

"He was proved guilty," Jane countered. "And he

will be treated as any person found guilty of treason." She looked to Reed for affirmation.

"We all can sympathize with your position, Holden," Reed said, leaning back in his chair with a heavy sigh.

Holden swallowed. Yes, the entire department knew Miko was Holden's twin brother, which was why the case had been given to Jane and not Holden.

He kept his gaze trained on their superior, effectively trying to ignore Jane's presence, which was near impossible. Pissed as hell would've been too mild of a phrase for the impotent rage choking him. He could admit Jane was a solid investigator, but he believed her final determination had been personal. Very personal. "Permission to remove Agent Fallon from the case for someone less biased."

Jane sputtered, and he could feel the force of her glare even though he kept his stare focused on Chief Harris. "Sir, I take offense to his accusation," she said. "My service record is impeccable, and I've given this office no reason to question my skills or my ability to separate my personal feelings from a case."

Chief Harris grunted in agreement, giving Holden a sour look that warned him to tread carefully. "Don't let your mouth overload your ass, son. Agent Fallon is more than qualified to handle this case. Permission denied. What's this about anyway?" He pushed the paperwork on his desk and tapped it with his stubbed finger. "Nothing is in this file that we all didn't already know was coming."

Jane had concluded that Miko had been guilty of

killing several people—including his own boss at the U.S. Department of Informational Development, or I.D. for short—and then committing suicide when the situation got too hot.

From the minute Holden had been told that Miko had killed himself at his own bar, something hadn't passed the sniff test. No way would Miko have committed suicide. Not in a million years. Honor was something the Archangelo boys held sacred, and there was nothing honorable about taking a coward's way out. "He didn't do it," he said between gritted teeth.

Jane shook her head, irritated. "Why are we having this conversation? I have eyewitness testimony that your brother ate a bullet. Harsh, yes, but sometimes the truth doesn't pull punches."

Holden had talked to Nathan Isaacs briefly about Miko's death and, though Nathan had been there when Miko died, this was not an open-and-shut case. As difficult as it was for Holden to accept that Miko had pulled the trigger, he could not believe the story ended there. "Something was missed. No one knew my brother like I did, and I'm telling you, something isn't right," he finished hotly.

"I'm sure the family members of most suicide victims share similar conviction, but I assure you, nothing was missed," Jane retorted, almost bored. "The truth is it doesn't matter how you feel about the matter, your brother did, indeed, kill himself and you're going to have to find a way to deal with that knowledge. It's time to face facts and move on. Miko Archangelo was found guilty of his crimes and, as per the regulations, will be stripped of all military honors effective immediately. Frankly, I find your outrage a little confusing. The report was finished a month ago."

"Yeah, and someone made sure that I'm just now seeing it," he shot back, leaving no doubt he believed it was Jane's doing. "Funny how that happened. If I'd known about your findings, I would've found a way to put a stop to your little celebration ceremony."

Jane colored but held her ground and looked to their superior to end the controversy once and for all. "Sir?"

Reed considered a moment and then said, "Son, I know you're hurting. You and your brother shared a close bond. But there comes a time when you have to accept the facts as they are given. Miko made a grave error in judgment and got in over his head. It's that simple. It hurts, I know, but we're not in the business of sugarcoating the truth."

Holden spied the tiniest lift of Jane's mouth and burned at the thought she might get the upper hand in this. Not because of their shared history—but because Miko's honor depended on Holden succeeding.

"I have new evidence," he blurted, taking a risk when he didn't have all his ducks lined up just yet. Jane frowned and opened her mouth to speak, but Holden wouldn't give her the chance to shoot him down. "Sir, I know I've got a dog in this fight, but that's all the more reason to let me at least see this through, whatever that end might be. Let me chase down this one lead, and if nothing comes of it, I'll let it go."

"This is ridiculous," Jane protested, shooting Holden a dark look. "The case is closed. What's next? Reopening every closed case when a family member squawks at the outcome? This sets the potential for a very dangerous precedent."

"If your investigation is solid, Jane, you have nothing to worry about," Holden returned. He couldn't give a rat's ass if Jane Fallon came out looking like a junior officer with her first real case. All he cared about was clearing Miko's name.

"And what's this new piece of evidence and why didn't you present it when Jane was conducting her investigation?" Reed asked. The older man watched him intently. "Did you purposefully withhold information in an attempt to protect your brother?"

"No sir. This information came to me only recently."

"What information is that?" Jane crossed her arms.

"It's my lead," he said coldly. "I'll chase it down. I wouldn't want your bias to color your judgment."

"My bias? What about yours?"

"If my brother is truly guilty, I'll close the book and let it be. I know he's not, though. If you had known my brother, you'd know he couldn't have done the things you say he did."

"And would you say your brother wasn't capable of gunning down innocent people? Because he absolutely did that," she countered. "That's irrefutable."

Holden swallowed. True, and that piece of the puzzle didn't make sense. All kinds of bad stuff had been happening under the auspices of I.D., which had subsequently been shut down, but Holden had a feeling the rot went even deeper than they'd uncovered. And somehow Miko had been at the heart of it.

"So spit it out," she pressed, her green eyes narrowing as she awaited his answer. "What's this new compelling evidence that miraculously appeared at the eleventh hour?"

He glanced at Reed. "I'd prefer to share that information in private."

His boss shook his head. "Jane is the investigating officer. Technically, any information you have should be shared with her, too." Reed's stare bounced from one officer to the other. "I really have no reservations with Jane as an investigator, nor do I feel she was biased. She followed the evidence and arrived at the conclusion that we all did." He drew himself up and effectively put an end to the conversation, saying, "I'm sorry, son, but this case is closed. You're going to have to make peace with it."

"My brother was a highly decorated marine." Holden's throat was tight. "To strip him of his medals... They were all he had left."

"He should've thought of that before he committed treason," Jane said, nodding to Reed with smug approval. "Sorry to have bothered you, sir."

Finished, she turned and left Holden standing in Reed's office, his anger smoldering so hot he didn't trust himself not to blow his entire career with one expletive. He reined in his anger enough to ask, "Sir, is that your final decision on the subject?"

"It is."

Holden accepted his superior's answer with a stiff nod and exited the office, but instead of going straight to his desk, he grabbed his coat and headed out. He needed air. Or else he was going to do something as foolish as throttle Jane Fallon.

From her desk, Jane watched Holden stomp out of the building. She released a pent-up breath. What possible evidence could Holden have that she hadn't uncovered in her investigation? She was known for her sharp eye and attention to detail. It wasn't possible she'd missed something. Right?

She returned to Reed's office, and her boss offered a brief, knowing smile. "He planted a seed, didn't he?"

"I didn't miss anything," she protested, but Reed was right; Holden had definitely planted a seed of doubt, and it was already germinating like a weed in her mind. "What do you think he was he talking about?"

"Does it matter?" Reed countered, and she supposed he was right. It didn't matter. The case was closed. "You have to understand that Holden is grieving the loss of his brother on several different levels. He'll survive this, and it will all become an unpleasant memory best left in the past."

She didn't think so. She'd known Holden for a year. They'd both transferred at the same time to the CIA, military affairs department, and ever since their brief, ill-fated and definitely secret affair, they'd been at odds with one another. However, if pressed, Jane would have to admit Holden was as thorough an officer as she—which meant if Holden thought he had new evidence, he likely did. "Maybe I ought to look into the case, make sure there aren't any loose ends."

Reed arched his brow. "You want to reopen it?" he asked.

"No," she said quickly. The last thing she wanted to do was reopen the case that had finally given her a measure of approval from her father, but if there was even the slightest chance she'd missed something, she couldn't let it go. "But I don't want Holden questioning my skills. I have no doubt that my investigation will hold up."

"Then why do you care what he thinks?"

"I don't." *I care what others will think if Holden starts spreading his theory around.* If word reached her father that she'd potentially buggered up the high-profile case.... She shuddered to think of how heavy his disappointment would be. "I just like to be thorough," she finished.

Reed sighed, as if knowing the exercise was pointless and a waste of manpower, but he shrugged and said, "Fine. I'll reopen the case for one week. But here's the catch," he added. "Holden is going to work with you."

"With all due respect, I don't think that's wise," she said, her heart skipping a beat. "He doesn't have a clear head. He's too emotional about this. Holden is a wild card that will only impede my progress."

"Potentially true, but Holden is a good officer—as good as you—and I have a feeling if he doesn't get the opportunity to chase this down, he's going to do something rash. I don't want to lose a good officer over this."

Work with Holden? She'd rather chew nails. "Sir, I can appreciate your concern but—"

"Decision is made. You and Holden have a week to get this cleared up. Try not to kill each other in the process."

And what if they did worse than kill each other? Jane's mouth dropped open in dismay, hating the idea of working side by side with Holden. From the minute they'd met, sparks had flown—the kind that made for incredible, earth-shattering sex but only made things messy everywhere else except the bedroom. She found him arrogant, harsh, cocky and too good-looking to be trusted. Anyone with eyes like his ought to be quarantined as a matter of national security. He was bad news. He reacted emotionally instead of rationally, and he didn't care how his actions affected other people. Such as when he wanted to come clean about their relationship and she wanted to keep it quiet. She had known her father would never approve, and she had told Holden this, which somehow had prompted him to have a conversation with her father, The Major. And that had gone down exactly as she'd imagined—not well. She'd ended her relationship with Holden and he had been adversarial with her ever since. Now whenever they were together, her armpits immediately started to sweat, which was why she'd switched to clinical-strength deodorant. He set her teeth on edge.

He also hogged the office exercise equipment. Of course, he would be the only other person who arose at a ridiculously early hour to get in a good workout before the day started. It was hard enough to forget his near-perfect body without having to exercise beside him each morning, but she was not about to purchase a gym membership when she had a free gym readily available to her.

And now she was supposed to work with him like they were buddies in a Sandra Bullock film? No way. Again, she'd rather eat nails. Rusty ones, at that.

She returned to her desk and glowered at her screensaver—flying blue stars streaking in wild patterns across her monitor. The pattern bothered her and she jiggled her mouse to make it stop.

"Why don't you just change your screensaver?"

Jane swiveled to stare at her officemate, Special Skills Officer Ursula Benza. "Because sometimes you have to assert your dominance over your OCD tendencies," she quipped before exhaling a short breath of annoyance at her situation. She frowned. "What do you know about Holden finding new evidence regarding his brother?" Ursula's blank look answered Jane's question. "Okay, so he didn't share," she surmised, not surprised. Holden was a locked box when he chose to be. "No idea what it could be?"

"Does anyone know what goes through that handsome head of his?" Ursula asked, smiling when Jane grimaced. "You're the only woman within a ten-mile radius who seems to be immune to his freakishly hot body, which begs the question about a certain lady's sexual orientation."

Jane shot Ursula a dark look. "Don't even go there. Maybe the reason I don't find him attractive is because he has the personality of a wet shoe." When it was obvious personality didn't matter to Ursula when presented with a hot male body, she added, "It would be inappropriate and weird to date a coworker." It was a good thing she wasn't overtly religious because the lie that just tripped from her mouth was entirely too convincing. Holden was her Achilles' heel and she was determined to root out that weakness.

"Hmm…who said anything about dating?"

Jane wrinkled her nose and Ursula grinned. Ugh. Knowing that her colleague harbored less than office-friendly fantasies about Holden made Jane twitch with discomfort. Okay, so it was complicated.

"So." Ursula tapped a finger on her desk. "What's this about more evidence about his brother's case?"

"I don't know. Holden wouldn't share, but Chief Harris put us both on the case just to be sure every stone has been checked and double-checked."

"Ouch. That's not going to go over very well with Daddy, is it?" Ursula guessed accurately, but Jane didn't want to think about it.

"My dad will understand this is just a formality. Nothing is going to change. Miko was guilty and that's what Holden will have to come to realize. Brother or not, Miko killed several people in cold blood and then offed himself. Sad but true."

"Brutal. Kind of makes you wonder why, though, right?"

"No." Jane disagreed sharply. "It's not my job to wonder about the motivations of criminals, and if this was anyone but Holden's twin brother, we wouldn't be having this conversation. Once again, his personal feelings are getting in the way."

"Can you blame the guy? I mean…family, you know? What if it was one of your brothers?"

"My brothers wouldn't shame their family by doing something like Miko did, so I can't imagine how I would feel. In my family, there are no shades of gray."

"Girl, you have a heart of stone." Ursula tsked with an arched brow. "Someday that quality is going to bite you in the ass."

"Not likely. However, I can definitely see Holden reaping terrible consequences if he keeps poking at the hornet's nest."

"So what are you going to do?"

The only thing she could do. "Put an end to this waste of time and prove once and for all that Miko Archangelo was a traitor to his country so we can all move on."

Case closed. Again.

Chapter 2

Holden was nursing a beer when he heard a knock at his front door. It was nearing eight o'clock in the evening. He grabbed his cell and checked his security camera feed, surprised and irritated when he saw Jane standing outside. "What the hell does she want? To gloat?" he muttered, pocketing his cell and going to the door, beer still in hand. He cracked the door and fixed her with a baleful stare that he hoped sent home the message she was the last person he wanted darkening his doorstep. "What do you want?" he asked, moving straight past the pleasantries to the point.

"Aren't you going to invite me in?" she asked. When he shook his head, her mouth firmed, but she didn't press the issue. Instead, she said, "Reed has agreed to reopen the case."

He straightened, surprised and immediately suspicious. "Why?"

She shrugged. "What does it matter? The case has been briefly reopened, and in the meantime, all disciplinary actions are pending the conclusion. However, there's a catch."

"Isn't there always?" he countered with a narrowed stare. "What is it?"

"Reed put me and you both on the case."

"Screw that."

"Exactly how I felt, but he's not going to change his mind."

"He will once he realizes that you and me working together is the worst idea since hydroponics."

"*Hydroponics?* You mean the world's first successful attempt at creating a sustainable way to grow food in a world with diminishing land resources? *That* hydroponics?"

"Yeah, exactly. Anything grown without dirt isn't natural. It's Frankenfood. So yeah, bad idea."

"Weird analogy aside, Reed has made up his mind, so we're working together on your fool's errand. Don't think for a second I believe you're operating on anything other than emotions and ignoring the facts—as usual. Frankly, I find your behavior an embarrassment to the department."

"Don't hold back. Let it all out, Agent Fallon," he said wryly, tipping his beer back and swallowing. "And since we're sharing, I should go on record as saying I think you're operating from a place of ego and fear because you're afraid you truly did miss something and you can't bear the thought of looking sloppy."

She lifted her chin with a cold grin. "Holden always has all the answers, doesn't he?"

"Most times. Particularly when the question isn't all that hard to figure out. Face it, Fallon. I've had you figured out from the day we met, and if you weren't so afraid of Daddy's disapproval, we could've been a helluva team."

"You're the one suffering from an inflated ego," she said, eyes flashing. "And I would appreciate it if you would stick to the case. Leave the personal crap out of this—that is, if you can manage."

"Cold as ice, as usual." His gaze darkened as he tipped his beer back again. "Tell me, Fallon, were you born this cold or did you work at it?"

She smiled. "I guess that's none of your business as it doesn't relate to the case. If you can't handle being a professional, I'll just let the chief know your interest in the case has died and we'll all happily close the book on this wild-goose chase."

He straightened, shaking his head. "You're a piece of work."

"As much as I would love to continue this conversation, I have a life and need to get back to it. I just came by to let you know you got your wish."

"Well, thank you for your consideration," he said with open sarcasm; he knew the real reason she'd dropped by was to get the slip of evidence he held to his chest. Good luck with that—he'd made it up. "Have a good evening, Agent Fallon."

She glared, standing rigid, looking as if she'd just sucked a lemon, but she forced a smile. "See you tomorrow. Be prepared to work. I want to get this over with. Some of us have real work to do and don't have time to chase fairy tales."

He chuckled. "Nice try, but I don't bait that easily. Good night, Fallon." He shut the door before she could retort. Work with Fallon? Nope. That woman was the original ice queen. And to think at one time he'd thought he was falling in love with her. What a joke. Besides, he worked alone. Fallon could do whatever she pleased as long as she stayed out of his way.

That'd gone about as well as she'd expected. But a girl could hope, right? Of course, she hadn't expected him to welcome her into his home with open arms and offer her a beer, but she hadn't quite expected him to be so rude. Well, yes she had. They weren't buddies, and she preferred it that way.

She walked with strong, purposeful strides to her car, suppressing a shiver at the bitter cold of a Washington, D.C., winter, and pushed the reality of working with Holden as far from her mind as possible. She was a strong investigator. Holden couldn't have anything in his hot little hand that would change the outcome of her investigation. And that was exactly what she'd tell her father in about fifteen minutes, when she was expected for dinner with her brothers.

There was a chance her father, retired Major General Gregory Fallon, hadn't heard of this recent development, but then her father still had scarily deep connections, and a reverberation of this sort was bound to ripple some water under the boats. However, if he didn't mention it, she'd keep the information to herself.

She walked into her father's house and followed the sound of voices to the living room, where her father and two brothers, Ian and Walker, sat enjoying a beer and talking shop. For a brief moment, a familiar envy arced across her heart for their easily defined relationships. Simply put, The Major was openly proud of his marine sons for their varied accomplishments, but when it came to his marine daughter, he always found cause to criticize. What would it be like to sit and enjoy a beer with her dad like her brothers did? The Major frowned upon women drinking—he said they lacked the constitution to handle their liquor. Yeah, her dad was unapologetically sexist and there was nothing she could do about it, least of all change him. Time to run the gauntlet. "Hey, Dad," she said, announcing herself as she entered the room.

"There she is, only a little bit late this time," The Major said with a wink at Ian, who laughed at her expense.

"Work kept me late," she said, hating the defensiveness of her tone. "Reed threw me a big case," she added, though she immediately wished she hadn't.

"Oh?" her older brother, Walker, said, intrigued. "Anything as good as that Archangelo case?"

Her dad grunted. "Those Archangelo boys, waste of good military training… Twisted branches never grow into strong oaks," he said, repeating the same bit of advice he'd shoved down her throat when he'd found out about her and Holden.

"Yes, Dad, I'm well aware of your feelings about Holden," she said, mildly irritated that she found herself defending the man. "But Holden is nothing like his brother—he's a good investigator with a solid record."

The Major shook his head. "The man has no respect for authority, which points to a weak character. Add in the fact that Miko was Holden's twin...mark my words, he'll show his true colors sooner or later."

Why was she wasting time defending Holden when she knew there was no winning this argument with her father? Total waste of energy. She'd long ago learned to pick her battles, and this situation was no different.

"So what's the big case?" Walker asked.

"I don't have details yet," she hedged. "I will know more in a few days." Her father narrowed a speculative gaze at her, as if he were reading her mind and discovering her secrets, and she suffered an uncomfortable moment. "When I can divulge details I will," she clarified. Anytime she tried to act as their equal, they managed to shoot her down with the equivalent of an indulgent pat on the head. Well, that was how her brothers handled it. Her father? He just got that look on his face that said, "Girl, you'll never be as good as your brothers because you're a woman and incapable of critical thinking" and she ended up doing and saying something that invariably started an argument. So tonight, she was determined to steer clear of any potential land mines. Yet…she'd just lobbed a big one in her own path. Self-destructive much? "I probably shouldn't have mentioned it."

The Major grunted and returned to his sons. "Walker, tell us about the latest detail in Afghanistan."

"Dad, you know I'm not supposed to talk about that—it's classified," he said, winking at their father. The Major laughed as if they were sharing a big private joke, and Jane hated she couldn't just enjoy an evening with her family like normal folks. Her thoughts wandered to Holden, and she pushed them back. She didn't want to think of him. Not now. She was already surrounded by big, tall, muscular numbskulls with too much testosterone. She certainly didn't need to muddy her brain with one more.

"Dad, how was the summit?" she asked, trying to steer the conversation. "Anything worth reporting?"

"Bunch of politicians jockeying to be top dog," he said. "Nothing new. Food was adequate for the situation, but I was more than happy to be home where a man can get a decent steak."

Adequate. Top chefs catered the military summit each year. It was mildly gratifying to know her father was difficult to please on all fronts. "Well, maybe you shouldn't be eating so much steak at your age," she countered. "Your cholesterol is probably through the roof."

"My cholesterol is fine," her dad said. Then his brow arched in a knowing fashion, and Jane's stomach flopped. He knew and he'd simply been waiting for a convenient segue. Damn the man's connections. He probably had a line to God so he knew when to pack an umbrella. "Let's get back on topic. Jane, an interesting conversation floated my way concerning the investigation you closed on that Archangelo man."

"Yes? Such as?" she asked, feigning polite interest when she really wanted to forgo eating and split this dinner invitation. She grabbed a handful of pretzels and tossed one back. "Anything good?"

"Talk is that his brother is asking questions."

"Well, that's not surprising. It was his brother after all," she answered, trying not to choke on the pretzel. "What's the big deal?"

"The big deal is the whole I.D. debacle was an embarrassment to this country and everyone is ready to put it to bed. You did a decent job closing that investigation to everyone's satisfaction. Perhaps you could persuade your peer to let sleeping dogs lie," The Major suggested, but his tone told her it was anything but. She hated when her dad pulled rank. "I.D. was a toxic extension of the government that ended up with gangrene. Many good people went down on that ship. No one wants to dredge it up again."

"I told him that," she said, biting her tongue too late. She looked to her brothers for help, but they were watching her as keenly as their father was. Damn boys. They stuck together, no matter what. Well, cat's out of the bag. No sense dancing around. She tossed back the last pretzel and said, "He's never going to stop asking questions. He doesn't believe Miko was guilty."

"The guy was caught red-handed," Ian said with a snort. "He couldn't have been more guilty than if he'd filmed himself doing it and mailed the evidence to the authorities."

"It's an open-and-shut case," Walker agreed. "I wish all my cases were that easy."

She bristled. "It wasn't that easy. The I.D. corruption went deep. There's always the potential we didn't root out all of the rot. I assure you, it wasn't an easy investigation by any means."

"Of course, Janey," Walker soothed in a patronizing way that made her want to sucker punch him in the kidneys. "It was a nice feather in your cap, for sure."

"Thanks, Walker," she gritted, her temperature rising. "Listen, I don't know if Holden has anything of value, but he says he has some new evidence."

Ian raised an eyebrow. "Like what?"

"I don't know," she admitted, hating that she'd blabbed at all. But no sense in hanging on to a half story. "Reed has temporarily reopened the case with Holden and me investigating."

Her dad scowled. "That's some special kind of bullshit. What possible evidence could this Holden character have that would warrant reopening the case?"

"I don't know, Dad," she answered truthfully. If only Holden hadn't been such a jerk and shared what he knew, she could've had solid answers, but now it seemed as if she were on the outside looking in on her own case. "I'm sure it's nothing truly substantial, but Reed thinks this will give Holden closure."

"Whole lot of hand-holding if you ask me." Her dad groused and her brothers nodded. "If I was in charge, none of that would be going on."

"Yes, Dad," she said dutifully, though she wanted to roll her eyes. Her dad had little faith that anyone could do their jobs as well as he could. Well, you didn't rise up the marine ranks by sitting back and letting the tide carry you. Her dad had the chops to back up his claims, but he wasn't the least bit gracious about it, which put him on the outs with almost everyone beneath him. "Anyway, I'm starved. When's dinner? I have an early day tomorrow and I still need to go over the case files."

"It should be ready now." Her dad motioned for everyone to follow him to the dining room. He nodded with brisk approval at Claudine, the live-in maid and cook, and then seated himself at the head of the table like a king surveying his subjects, which Jane thought was an apt analogy.

"Smells great, Claudine," she murmured, ready to dig in and get the hell out.

"How are you, Miss Jane?" Claudine asked, placing the gravy boat nearest to her father because he practically drank the stuff with a straw. Her father was waging a war against time, determined to prove he was damn near invincible, no matter that he was nearing seventy.

"Good, and yourself?"

"Can't complain." The older woman smiled. "When are you going to meet a nice young man?"

"No time for that," she said briskly, shaking her head as she scooped a spoonful of mashed potatoes. Why didn't anyone ever ask why Walker or Ian hadn't settled down? Because men were allowed to be footloose and fancy-free, she answered herself in a sour tone. "I'm married to my job," she said, thinking briefly of the time she and Holden had spent together. If things had been different…maybe…but they weren't, so what was the point in wallowing in the past?

Her father nodded and said, "There's more to life than getting married, Claudine. Don't be putting foolish thoughts into the girl's head. She's *finally* doing all right. Time to focus on the priorities."

Somehow having her father echo the same sentiment sent a stone tumbling into the pit of her stomach when it should've made her grin from ear to ear. She was constantly yearning for a smidgeon of her father's approval, yet sometimes the smidge just tasted hollow.

Hell, she must be tired. This whole situation with Holden and the case had put her off-kilter. Tomorrow she'd find out what the hell kind of evidence Holden thought he had and then she'd start putting this baby to bed. For good.

Chapter 3

Per usual, Holden awoke at 4:30 a.m., and after pounding back an organic whey protein shake, dressed, grabbed his workout bag and headed for the office.

Being in the top level of the CIA had its perks, one of them being the executive exercise facility, which Holden took full advantage of. After a career in the military, he didn't relish the idea of going soft at a desk job, so he worked out just as hard as he ever did. And also, per usual, Jane was there, too.

It was always a small punch to the gut whenever he saw Jane dressed like a civilian in her workout clothes. It reminded him too vividly how that lithe, muscular body had fit so well against his, and it was in those raw, primal moments that his guard slipped, if only for a heartbeat. And then he remembered how she'd thrown his feelings in his face and walked out on him and the wall went back up.

"Would it kill you to exercise at a different time?" he asked as she joined him, stuffing her bag in the locker and grabbing a towel. "Or is this some twisted scheme to spend more time with me?"

"Don't flatter yourself."

He didn't know why he'd assumed she'd cut out on her morning workout after getting the news that the case had been reopened, but obviously it hadn't stopped her. Seeing her there put him instantly on edge.

She headed directly to the treadmill and punched in her usual workout, a punishing ten-mile run in fifty-five minutes. Holden, deciding to bypass his lifting routine, stepped onto the treadmill beside her. He punched in ten miles and kicked up the pace.

After they'd started running, Holden asked, "So why'd Reed change his mind? You have something to do with that?"

"What does it matter?"

"It matters to me."

She cut him a short look. "I don't like my work to look sloppy. I realized that if you think you have hard evidence, chances were you did, and I didn't want to run the risk that someone else might question my skills as an investigator. I figured chasing down the lead was a minimally small risk when I feel confident the end result will remain the same."

"Why are you so willing to believe the worst of my brother?"

"I didn't know your brother, so I have no opinion of him. I followed the evidence. Your brother's death was the catalyst to the entire I.D. network becoming a pile of rubble. That much is easy enough to document. Your brother was implicated in the killings of several high-ranking officials internationally, as well as domestically, and his suicide—"

"*Alleged* suicide," he interrupted with a growl, and she shrugged, keeping an easy but brisk pace without breaking a sweat. She was in remarkable shape. One would have to be blind not to notice—and Holden was not blind. Not to mention he had first-hand knowledge of every curve and valley carved into that hot body. "And Nathan Isaacs, his good friend and fellow sniper for I.D., had also been accused of committing unsanctioned hits, and he wasn't stripped of his medals."

"Nathan didn't know he was carrying out someone else's agenda. Miko did. That much was said in his suicide note."

"We don't even know the note was written by Miko because it was printed out and not handwritten. For all we know, my brother was set up by someone higher up the chain."

"How high are we talking?" she asked, a faint note of mockery in her tone. "C'mon, Holden, Occam's razor. Sometimes the most obvious explanation is the right one."

"And sometimes what may seem like the obvi-

ous answer is in actuality what someone wants you
to believe."

"Well, you got your wish. We're going to chase
down your lead and see where it takes us. Just don't
blame me when we end up in the same place we
started."

He knew it was possible Jane was right, but his gut
said otherwise. He couldn't explain the twin bond to
someone who'd never experienced it. But he could
chase down a lead like a bloodhound, and that was
what he was going to do. He supposed he owed Reed
a note of gratitude for opening the door so he could
walk through instead of having to scale windows in
the dead of night. Sneaking around wasn't his favorite game.

"So what's your story, Fallon?" he asked, curious
as to what went on behind those jade eyes.

She shot him an irritated look. "Are you going to
gab all morning or let me run in peace? You'll have
plenty opportunity to flap your jaws later."

"I forgot that your workout takes all your con-
centration," he said, knowing the subtle jab would
ruffle her feathers. From what he knew of Jane, she
didn't take shortcuts and didn't do girl push-ups. In
fact, she worked harder than most men. She was a
marine through and through. As expected, she cast
him a dark look and punched in a higher pace as if
to prove a point. He chuckled and did the same. They
were running side by side, like a cheetah and a ga-
zelle, except they were evenly matched in skill and
strength. Sweat began to drip down his temple and

soak his T-shirt. A quick look at Jane revealed high points of color pinching her cheeks as she kept up the pace. At this rate, their hearts would explode, and she was so damn stubborn she'd never quit before him. He didn't want to show weakness, but running had never been his strong suit. Her legs pumped, strong and fierce, as she kept her gaze trained forward, and he had to wonder where she went in her head to withstand such a grueling workout. Running was a mental activity as much as it was physical and Jane was in the zone. He envied her detachment, her ability to compartmentalize the pain of her burning legs and lungs as she pushed herself beyond most people's capability. Maybe that was how she had been able to just cut him loose and walk away without looking back. *Don't start that crap again,* a sharp voice in his head warned when he went too deep into the whys of their breakup. *Ancient history—keep it there.*

Just when he thought he might collapse, the ten-mile marker dinged and the slowdown began, not a moment too soon. Another five seconds and he might've embarrassed himself. His legs were rubber, but he wasn't about to let Jane see that, particularly when she looked ready to go another five miles. The only indication she'd labored was the ruddy color in her cheeks and the quick rise and fall of her chest as she wiped away the sweat. She ended the run and popped off the treadmill, calling over her shoulder before she headed for the showers, "Be ready to share this game-changing lead, Archangelo. Time is wasting."

* * *

Jane stood for a full two minutes under the hot spray, groaning silently at the dull ache in her quads and calves from the grueling run. Why'd she have to push it so hard? What did she need to prove to Holden? It wasn't just Holden—it was to everyone. There was no grace for her. Being the only girl in a military family dominated by men, she'd had no choice but to meet or exceed all expectations. Hell, she'd been doing boy-style push-ups since she was three. She loved her brothers to death, but they were jarhead carbon copies of their dad, and because she was the exact opposite of her father, it must mean she was her mother's mini me. She stifled another groan. Why couldn't she have been born a male, too? Life would've been so much simpler. No having to constantly prove her worth or justify her existence. No having to defend the fact that she'd been born bearing a striking resemblance to their mother.

The mother who'd left them all behind.

Sometimes she bore her mother's abandonment as a scarlet letter simply because she had the misfortune to share the same gender.

Jane indulged in a moment of quiet as the water soothed her throbbing muscles and calmed her ragged spirit. Why was she going on this stupid waste of time with Holden? Why didn't she just stand her ground and discard Holden's theory? There was no basis of fact, only Holden's insistence that something was amiss, and that wasn't enough to reopen a case like Miko's. Why? The question pelted her as surely as the water jets, but there was no relief answer in sight. Jane groaned, hating the self-doubt niggling at her brain, cutting chunks out of her confidence. Maybe she should've gone to Holden when she had first started the investigation. Perhaps if she'd done that, they wouldn't be questioning anything now, putting a stain on her reputation. But then, as now, she didn't trust herself around Holden for too long; he did something to her insides. Too much time around Holden and she started to question too many things, and she couldn't have that. He put a wrinkle in her life that stubbornly refused to iron out, no matter how hard she pressed. And that just wouldn't work in the overall scheme of things. *Enough of this morose, angst crap.* She pushed away from the spray and grabbed the soap. *It's not as if things are going to change.*

She'd have to put some ointment on her calves tonight, she realized, twisting her foot in a circular motion and grimacing at the immediate protests in her muscles. That was what she got for trying to show off.

But Holden could handle the challenge, she realized with grudging respect. Most people would've quit the minute she upped the pace. A secret part of her was glad he hadn't. She couldn't respect a man who couldn't keep up with her. Did she want Holden's respect? Why should that play into the equation? Jane had to admit, something about Holden made her want to look twice in his direction. She'd seen plenty of hard bodies during her military career—so much so it was more surprising to see a soft physique— but Holden's body was carved from granite, all hard planes and razor sinews of strength that made her itch to touch them. Just admitting that to herself sent shameful heat scuttling to her cheeks, and she actually heard her father's voice in her head ranting about "female hormones" and the pursuant "unstable" nature of all women.

Get a grip, Fallon. Stay focused on the big picture. Protect your reputation in the department and find a way to show Holden he's wrong about his brother.

She shut off the water and wrapped her towel around her with a grim smile. Sounded like a solid plan. *Now get to it.*

Chapter 4

Fifteen minutes later both Holden and Jane were alone in the conference room ready to work. Despite the fact she'd just run a grueling distance and had just hopped out of the shower, Jane looked impeccable, dressed in a tailored suit and her short, dark hair blown dry and styled. Holden, however, could still feel water dripping down his back from the quick towel off and subsequent dash to the office. Suddenly, he felt disheveled. He shifted in discomfort at the pull of his shirt beneath his suit jacket and took a seat opposite Jane.

She got right to it. "Okay, Holden, here's your chance. What's this new evidence you're talking about?"

Time to come clean. "I lied." He watched as a

storm immediately sprang to life in her eyes. He held his hands up in a conciliatory gesture, hoping to ward off the lightning before she incinerated him where he stood. "I knew that if I said I just had a gut feeling, there's no way anyone would've taken me seriously."

"You lied?" Her voice registered cold disbelief as she stiffened. Jane skewered him with her gaze, saying in a low whisper, "I knew it."

"Let me explain," he started, but she wasn't interested in his reasons, not that he blamed her. Anyway, he didn't really care about her opinion of him.

"This only further proves my point," she said, waving off his attempt. "You are definitely not thinking clearly if you are willing to jeopardize your entire career for a disgraced brother who'd made his own bed." She rose abruptly. "I'm telling Reed. This farce of an investigation is finished."

"Wait," he said, compelling her to stop. "Reed has agreed to let us investigate, to dig a little deeper. What will it hurt to flip over a few more stones?"

"What will it hurt? *My credibility.* I know it seems crazy to think of someone aside from yourself, but I have a personal interest in seeing this case closed. This was my case and I investigated it to its successful conclusion. Just because you don't like the outcome doesn't mean you get to change the ending of the story. With your military background, I'm surprised you would sink this low."

Maybe he should've made something up. But a small voice inside his head had urged him to be truthful. He'd thought maybe if he could convince Jane he was right, she'd be a powerful ally. But now he was thinking that voice was insane and had definitely steered him wrong. Holden recalled another time he'd listened to that little voice and it'd blown up in his face—the time he'd told Jane he loved her and wanted to build a life with her. She couldn't dump him fast enough. Yeah, when was he going to learn to tell that voice to shut the hell up?

Time for damage control before things went sidewise fast. "I shouldn't have lied, but look at it from my point of view. I can't explain to you a twin bond because frankly, I don't understand it myself. But my brother and I knew each other like we knew ourselves. My brother was involved in something bigger than what we've seen. We've only scratched the surface of what's really going on. I know this as strongly as I know that I can't stand peas." He shrugged. "It's an ingrained knowledge. We have a week to figure out what really happened. If you truly believe my brother is guilty, how will giving me that one week to chase down any leads hurt your case? If I'm wrong, I'm wrong. Nothing changes. But if I'm right—and I believe I am—there's so much more at stake than my brother's honor."

"Such as?"

"If someone else was pulling the strings, then the real threat is still out there. And it's our job to find it and neutralize it."

Jane frowned. "I did my job, and now you want to come along and tear it apart just to soothe an emotional wound? I'm sorry, but I can't do that."

"What if it was one of your brothers?" he asked.

She shook her head. "It wouldn't be. My brothers would never do anything so rogue. You and I both know that I.D. was on the fringe. Your brother was attracted to that department because of who he was. He was an adrenaline junkie who craved excitement and glory. And I.D. gave it to him. He didn't care where it came from as long as he got his fix."

"You didn't know Miko, so don't pretend you wrote the book on his character analysis. I'm telling you right now, the man you just described was not my brother. He liked to play the hero, that much is true, and he truly thought he was doing good work. He was doing the jobs that others couldn't to keep his country safe. I'm sure he was devastated when he found out I.D. had played him false."

"So devastated he kept putting people in his gun sights and collecting those paychecks?" she mocked. Holden understood she was not buying one red cent of his plea. "You're spinning your wheels. Your brother screwed up and you're screwing up by championing a lost cause."

"A man of my brother's character would never pull the trigger on himself unless he was forced to," Holden stated matter-of-factly, ignoring her mockery. "He just wouldn't. Someone forced his hand. Aren't you the least bit curious—no, *worried*—about who is actually calling the shots? I owe it to my brother to figure things out, but *you* owe it to our country. I know that means something to you. We can't protect

our nation from outside threats if we can't even iden-
tify what threats may reside right in our own house."

He was reaching her—he could see it in her eyes.
"I don't like your methods," she finally said, looking as if she'd rather eat rat guts than admit he may
have a point, but she wasn't stupid and that was a
point in her favor. "You shouldn't have lied. Good,
bad or indifferent, you should've taken your chances
with the truth."

"Maybe. But what's done is done and I'm not about
to apologize. Are you with me or are you going to
turn tail and run back to the chief to tattle on me?"

Her lips pressed together in a tight line. She
didn't like being called a tattler. "Fine," she snapped.
"You've got one week. If at the end of the week we
don't have anything substantial to go on, we're closing this case and I never want to hear about it again.
Am I clear?"

"Crystal." He breathed a sigh of relief. If Jane had
marched into Reed's office and told their superior that
Holden had misrepresented the facts, he could have
been fired. It was a gamble he'd begrudgingly been
willing to take. Having Jane on his side would make
things a lot easier by half. Well, the investigating
process would go more smoothly. Now he just had to
find a way to stop thinking of her in terms that had
nothing to do with the job. *Focus, man.* "Since we've
sorted that out, I want to stop by my brother's bar. He
spent the most time there. We might find evidence."

"We went over the place with a fine-tooth comb.
There's nothing there. Besides, everything's been

packed up and stored in evidence. The bar is nothing but an empty shell. Plus, it's been put up for sale to satisfy debts levied against your brother's estate."

"I know all that. But I want to go anyway. I feel as if we missed something. If I know my brother, he left information behind."

Jane crossed her arms. "This is a waste of time. If you'd like, we can go through the evidence collected, but I don't relish the idea of traipsing around an empty bar, especially when there's no heat and it's snowing outside."

"You can go where you choose, but I'm heading to the bar." He scooped up his notebook and stuffed it into his satchel. It was hard to get used to—carrying the equivalent of a man purse—but it served its purpose.

She scowled. "Fine. I suppose since this whole investigation is a wild-goose chase, what's one more stop?" She grabbed her coat and slipped it on. "Any other ridiculous stops we'll be making along the way? Perhaps you'd like to get a latte while we're at it?"

"A latte sounds like a great idea," he shot back with a smirk. "I knew you were good for something." The glare she sent his way only made him grin wider. He really shouldn't enjoy ruffling her feathers, but when it was so easy…he couldn't help but grab the low-hanging fruit.

As they drove to Miko's former bar, Holden realized he needed to smooth things over if he and Jane were going to work together. Fact was, as much as he hated it, he needed her help and he wasn't going to get it by constantly needling her. "Listen, I'm sorry about the latte joke. I have mad respect for your investigative skills. And if that didn't come across when we first started this relationship, I apologize. Believe it or not, I was considered the smooth-talking brother." When his joke fell flat, he sighed. "C'mon, is this what it's going to be like for the next week? Shouldn't we at least *try* to get along?"

"You're asking me to willingly tear apart my own investigation to satisfy some gut instinct that your brother wasn't the bad guy, and you expect me to be happy about it? You're questioning my skills as an investigator. Sorry if that doesn't make me feel all warm and fuzzy."

"I remember what made you feel warm and fuzzy," he said, mostly to himself, but he enjoyed the sudden flush in her cheeks, which told him she remembered, too.

She cut him a dark look. "Keep the jokes to yourself, Archangelo. I'm certainly not in the mood for your bullshit."

He chuckled. "What a ball buster. Your family must be so proud. Tell me, Fallon, when was your father aware he had *three* sons instead of two?"

"I hate to break it to you, but you suck at stand-up comedy. Perhaps an alternative career in sanitation would be more suited for your skill set."

"Ouch. Sanitation…that's brutal. Are you calling me a piece of shit or just implying I'm only good for cleaning it up?"

"Take your pick." She shrugged.

Damn, this was gonna be one long week.

Jane was fuming. If she were a cartoon character, heat waves would've been steaming from the top of her head. She hated how Holden had manipulated her into opening this case, when in fact there'd been no true reason to do so. Now if she went to Reed and admitted she'd fallen for Holden's bait, she'd end up looking like the weak-minded investigator who had no confidence in her skills. And now he was trying to joke? Even worse, bring up their sexual history? Who the hell did he think he was? She found nothing funny about the situation and she sure as hell didn't appreciate him throwing in an inappropriate sexual reference. If she thought she could get away with it, she might've unloaded a clip into his numbskull. "What do you hope to find at the bar?" she asked in a clipped tone. "And if you thought there was something at the bar, why didn't you look before now?"

"Because I wasn't thinking clearly after I heard the news about my brother. It's called grief."

Oh, good gravy. She had to let that pass or else she'd end up looking like a heartless bitch. "Don't you think if you had such a tight bond with your brother he would have told you he was in some kind of trouble?"

"Yes." He nodded but added, "Unless he thought doing so would put me in danger. A few months before he died, he'd been acting really strange. Evasive. Twitchy, even. If I hadn't known better, I would've said he was doing drugs, but my brother was against illegal substances. We'd both seen too many good soldiers get messed up by meth or heroin. My brother would never touch that shit."

"But if you were so close, why didn't you try to pin him down and get the answers?"

"I tried. By that point, my brother must've been in too deep and I couldn't reach him. At the time, I thought Miko was just going through a weird phase and maybe needed some space. It happens with twins—going your whole life attached to another human being, you sort of lose your own identity—so I figured it might be something like that. But it wasn't, and by the time I realized something bad was about to happen he was dead."

"And you have no idea what he could've been into?"

"No. His work with I.D. was classified, and honestly, I didn't think I needed to care. It wasn't until he started acting weird that I realized maybe I ought to poke my nose where it didn't belong."

"And what makes you think Miko didn't know what he was doing?"

He shrugged. "I don't know. Maybe he did, but he was trapped by circumstance. Sometimes when you're knee-deep in mud and you're sinking fast, your first and only thought is staying alive. Maybe that's what happened."

That was a lot of *maybe.* "You're going to need a lot more than flimsy theory to make any meaningful change to your brother's file. Unfortunately, brotherly love doesn't supersede the facts."

He bristled with mild insult. "Of course not. I would never expect it to, but when you have a man who has lived his life by a certain code of honor and prides himself on being someone you can respect, ignoring the clues to dig deeper is just lazy investigating."

Did he just call her lazy? The man had balls. "Do not *ever* call me lazy. Just because you're having a hard time accepting facts doesn't mean you get to throw my skills under the bus. I went above and beyond to find the answers. More was at stake than just your brother's life. High-ranking officials were killed, and I.D.'s rot caused the disintegration of an *entire* department. I'd say more than your brother's *honor* was destroyed."

"You're right," he conceded, but followed by saying, "but my brother's honor is all that I care about."

Jane knew he spoke with raw honesty. He'd do anything to prove his brother's innocence, which made her wonder—would he be willing to lie to save his brother's ass? She'd have to keep a close eye on him.

Holden might be just as dangerous as Miko in an entirely different way.

Chapter 5

Reed Harris shook hands with his unexpected visitor, curious as to why Ulysses Rocha, one of the owners of Tessara Pharmaceuticals, had requested an audience. Ulysses, who, also with extensive military experience, had turned to the private sector for more lucrative opportunities; and in spite of the negative press incurred by the situation involving Penelope Granger, another high-profile shareholder, Tessara Pharm was still turning a substantial profit.

"Forgive me, but what is this about?" he asked, getting straight to the point. Ulysses, a barrel-chested man with eyes as hard as flint, cracked a smile that looked entirely out of place on his face, making Reed wonder what the hell was truly going on. "It isn't every day that I receive requests for a meeting outside of certain circles."

"I can appreciate that. As you know, Tessara Pharm has suffered a number of unfortunate events lately, most notably with one of our major founders, Penelope Granger, aka Penny Winslow, who was found guilty of running I.D. as her own personal hit squad through her association with Tom Wyatt."

"Yes, I am aware," Reed said. "Corruption is an equal-opportunity contaminant."

"Yes, so it would seem. Tessara Pharm has suffered its fair share of bad press, and as such, we would be happy to leave all that sordid business in the past, as you can well imagine."

"Of course."

"So when we heard the case involving Miko Archangelo had been reopened, we were concerned how that might affect Tessara Pharm."

Ah…the true reason for the visit. "These things happen. New evidence cropped up and we're obligated to follow the trail wherever it may lead."

"New evidence?" At Reed's noncommittal nod, Ulysses frowned. "What possible new evidence could there be? Both Penny and Miko are dead and I.D. has been shut down."

"Let's put a pin in that question for a moment and draw attention to a question I have—how exactly do you have knowledge of a classified investigation? As far as I'm aware, Tessara Pharm is not on the executive payroll…or is it?"

A slow, cold smile spread across his face, as if

amused that Reed was questioning him. That alone was enough to get the man thrown out, but something stayed Reed's hand. Something wasn't right and it wasn't just that Ulysses was trying to pry information out of him.

The man cocked his head to the side. "Let's just say that people in high places have expressed an interest in seeing that the Archangelo case remains closed. People need to be able to move on, Chief Harris. Surely you understand that?"

Reed didn't like the man's tone. A shiver of warning played "Taps" on his spine. He clasped his hands carefully atop his desk and waited. Again that cold smile appeared.

"There is no conspiracy," Ulysses continued. "No big cover-up. Just businesspeople concerned that dredging up bad history will lead to a bad future for their bottom line. Shareholders are sensitive to fluctuations in their dividends. It's our job to make sure those dips and valleys aren't too sharp."

"And it's my job to make sure the security of our nation isn't at risk," Reed countered smoothly. "Frankly, I could give two shits about your shareholders' bottom line, and you have some balls to come in here and expect me to dance to your tune just because you *know* a few people. Well, newsflash...I know a few people, too."

"I see." Ulysses dropped the smile, which was fine by Reed; they both knew it was fake. "I guess it'll have to come down to who knows the better people."

He laughed. "I answer to the president. Who do

you answer to? A bunch of entitled rich people? I think I win."

Ulysses rose and adjusted his suit coat. "I'd hoped we could see eye to eye on this."

"I don't see how we could," Reed said with frank amusement. "We seem to be on opposite continents."

"So it would seem."

Ulysses showed himself to the door and walked out without further comment. It wasn't until Ulysses had left the building that Reed let out his held breath. Something foul was afoot. It would appear Holden was right; there was more to the story than met the eye. Was Miko simply a pawn in a bigger game? And if so, who was the true game master? The entire situation left a bad taste in his mouth, but he had no doubt if there was something to be found, Holden would find it.

Reed's only fear? Miko had already paid for his involvement with his life. Reed sure as hell didn't want his two best agents to pay the same price.

The Realtor, none too happy to be out in the blustery weather with two people who plainly weren't going to be buying, opened the front door of the bar and stamped his feet free of the snow clinging to his boots. "Two floors. The upstairs was the office area." He looked at his watch. "Do you know how long this is going to take?"

"You can wait in your car if you prefer," Holden suggested and the Realtor was only too happy to take him up on his suggestion.

After the man had disappeared, Holden and Jane clicked on their flashlights, illuminating the dim interior. The bar had been closed for almost six months, but the stale smell of beer remained. Holden had visited a few times right after Miko purchased it. It was supposed to be the thing that kept him busy after retirement, he recalled, the memory springing to mind...

"A bar?" Holden had exclaimed as Miko drove them to the location for the first time. "You bought a bar?"

"Yeah, sounded like a good idea at the time," Miko had said, grinning. "What could be better than being the proprietor of good times? I figure I might as well make a little money at the place where I most often frequent on my downtime, right?"

"Owning a bar is more than just free beer, Miko," Holden had said, frowning. "It's a huge responsibility."

"Stop being such a wet blanket. Things are good. I'm no longer punching a clock and I've landed a pretty sweet side gig, so I can afford to lose money on the bar for years before I start to sweat. And if it gets to be too much of a pain in the ass, I'll just unload it. So stop worrying."

Holden had glanced around the bar, grudgingly noting the whiskey-soaked charm of the place, and he'd realized his brother could make a killing if managed properly. But Miko was all about the good time, not the profit margin. He had thought then that even if Miko put minimal effort into the bar, it'd still turn a profit, which had been reassuring. Good location, clean but not too pristine, with a lived-in, comfortable feel. Like the bar in that show *Cheers*. Where everyone knew your name. He had looked to Miko, who had still been awaiting his opinion, and said with a smile, "Tell me about this side gig." Miko had just shaken his head and hooked his arm around Holden's shoulders.

"First, we celebrate. Life is good, my brother. Life is good."

As Miko's voice faded from Holden's memory, his eyes stung. "You okay?" Jane asked, peering at him. "You look as if you're going to cry."

"I'm fine," he said roughly, heading toward the staircase, then taking the steps two at a time. He detoured to the left and opened the door to Miko's private office with Jane on his heels. To her credit, she didn't pester him to share his feelings, and he was grateful. His grief over the death of his twin was something he kept close to his heart and covered with plenty of layers—he didn't have the luxury of breaking down. The hardwood floor creaked beneath their feet and echoed in the nearly empty room. Everything of value had been stripped from the walls and sold at auction. Only Miko's desk remained for staging purposes. A small, high window let in cold, milky light, but the gloom in the room seemed to seep into Holden's bones. A sense of danger clung to the shadows, and he pushed the disquieting sensation away so he could focus.

It seemed he wasn't the only one keying in on the

weirdness in the room. "The mind plays tricks on you when you know someone died violently in the space you're in," Jane said, rubbing at her arms and shivering inside her thick jacket. "But even still, this place is giving me the creeps. Can we get on with it before hypothermia hits?" She glanced around with irritation. "I don't even know what we're looking for."

"Anything."

"Well, thank you for that completely unhelpful direction." She gestured to the still room. "Nothing's here. Everything's been cleaned out, either to sell or to put into evidence."

She wasn't saying anything that Holden couldn't see for himself, but his gut told him that something was here. *Show me, Miko. If you're in this room, watching me stumble around in the dark...give me something to go on....*

He crossed to the desk and began opening the drawers, the old wood scraping against the rollers with a screech. A few pens rolled out along with a puff of dust and an assortment of discarded paper clips. He picked up one of the pens and shone the light on the lettering. Tessara Pharm. Not surprising, since it had been discovered Penelope Granger, aka Penny Winslow, was the one pulling the strings. He pocketed the pen and closed the drawer.

Jane caught the movement and moved toward him. "What's that and why are you putting it in your pocket?"

"Calm down. It's a pen."

"Why are you taking it?"

"Because I am."

She let it go, which was good. He didn't know why he had scooped up the pen, either. "Where's it from?" she asked.

"Tessara Pharm."

"Ugh. That place leaves a bad taste in my mouth. Big pharm companies are usually up to no good, in my opinion."

"Yeah, I hear you," he agreed, moving to the next drawer and opening it. Empty. He slid his hand along the edge of the bottom, looking for anything that his brother might've hidden, but nothing aside from wood met his fingers. Dropping to his knees, he flashed the light beneath the desk, checking for evidence of a false bottom, but he saw nothing out of the ordinary. He rose with sharp disappointment, feeling as if he were missing what was right in front of him.

He thought Jane sensed his disappointment, though for a long moment, she didn't say anything. "I understand—" she began, and he immediately cut her off.

"You don't understand, and don't patronize me with your attempt," he said brusquely, moving away from the desk and flashing the light into the corners of the room.

"I'm just trying to help," she muttered.

"Yeah, well, help by looking. There's something here. I can feel it."

"Great—another gut instinct. Does your gut give a clue as to where exactly we should be looking, because all I see is a sad empty room that's as cold as a storage locker."

Frustration built under his breastbone. "Hell, I don't know," he said, walking slowly over the floorboards to listen for minute changes. He walked into the small supply closet and flashed the light around. Nothing but empty shelves and dust. He stamped the floor, listening for a sound change. He explained when he caught Jane watching him with a question in her gaze. "When Miko and I were kids, we would hide things in the floorboards of our old house. We were always trying to hide alcohol or important stuff from our old man, who was a raging alcoholic. When he was sober, he was an okay dad, but when he drank…let's just say he made living hard." He didn't know if Miko had held on to the habit, but it was worth a shot.

"How often did your dad drink?" she asked.

"Only on the days that ended in *Y*."

"Sorry." She seemed to mean it. "So what'd you hide?"

"Anything we didn't want him to sell or break. Sometimes we hid money, too. Otherwise, our dad would drink it all away and we'd have nothing left for food."

"That's rough."

He shrugged. "Everyone's got a sob story, right?"

"Yeah, I suppose."

"How about yours? I can only go from what I know firsthand, but your dad seems like a piece of work. Couldn't have been easy growing up with The Major."

"Oh, is this sharing time?" She lifted her brow. When he hiked his shoulder, she shook her head, not ready to reciprocate. "Let's just focus on the task at hand, all right?"

"I'm curious.... How happy was your dad when you broke things off with me? He probably threw a ticker-tape parade."

"My dad doesn't like showy extravagances," she answered, flashing her light along the ceiling, looking anywhere but at Holden. "And he'd never do anything that gave anyone the impression you mattered in the overall scheme of things."

"What was his problem? As far as I know, I never pissed in his cornflakes."

"Are we doing this now?" she asked, annoyed. "It's in the past and we're here to do a job. Story hour will have to wait."

"Suit yourself." He shrugged and continued to slowly pan the floor. Why was he looking for answers to a mystery that didn't need solving? Who cares if some self-important asshole didn't think he was good enough for his daughter? "But here's the thing, you dropped me like a bad habit all because Daddy said so. Frankly, Fallon, I thought you had bigger balls than that."

She stopped and met his gaze. "My balls, or lack thereof, are none of your business. Can we please stick to the task at hand, or would you rather pull up a chair and start a counseling session? I should warn you, I'm all out of tissues."

"You're a piece of work. You did me a favor," he

muttered, unable to believe he'd opened his mouth in the first place. "Forget I mentioned it."

"Already have."

Damn, he was stupid ten times over for bringing up ancient history at the worst possible time. But sometimes his mouth just took over and he had to run to catch up. Sort of like the day he'd taken it upon himself to have a talk with The Major. Yeah, that'd ended in all sorts of bad. He supposed good intentions didn't mean crap in the Fallon household. Holden's first real, solid relationship had gone down in flames all because some crotchety five-starred major general had really messed up ideals and expectations for his only daughter.

Holden looked at Jane. "You know, I feel sorry for you." Jane regarded him with a wary expression, but he continued. "Yeah, I do, because you're constantly looking for Daddy's approval and you've obviously never seen the movie before. Well, I have, and I can tell you—it never ends the way you want it to. Your dad is an overbearing prick and he'll never give you what you're looking—no, begging—for, yet you'll sacrifice everything in your life for that one tiny nugget of approval from a man who ought to just love you for who you are. And it's sad, Fallon. Really sad."

She swallowed audibly and he knew he'd hit a nerve, but in true Fallon style, she didn't bend or show weakness. "Are you finished?" she asked in a husky tone that immediately made him feel like a toad. What the hell was wrong with him? He should've just left it alone. What did it matter what her issues with her dad were? They didn't affect him any longer. Jane was free to live under her father's thumb if she chose.

He waved her off. "Forget it. I don't know what's come over me. I'm sorry...that was out of line. I guess I'm just on edge."

"Sure." She accepted his apology with a stiff nod and walked away as they both continued to search the office.

After ten minutes, Holden rose with a muttered expletive. "You're right, nothing's here."

"I'll meet you downstairs," Jane said, heading for the door. Although she had a reputation for being a hard-nosed investigator, she was plainly happy to get out of the room. Seemed Jane wasn't immune to the heebie-jeebies.

Holden took one final look at his brother's office, trying not to picture him sprawled across his desk with the back of his head shot off. Nathan had said in his statement that moments prior to Miko eating that bullet, he had told Nathan to dig deeper into Tessara Pharm. Nathan Isaacs, one of Miko's best friends and fellow snipers formerly employed by the now-defunct I.D., had managed to peel back a layer of corruption within the covert government agency, but he'd nearly died in the process.

Holden caught up with Jane on the stairs. "I didn't see any mention of Tessara Pharm in your report aside from the brief notation about Winslow. Didn't you ask any questions regarding Miko's involvement with the pharm company?"

"What involvement? Winslow was the only con-nection to Tessara Pharm, and she's dead, which I noted in my report."

"The last thing my brother said to Nathan Isaacs was for him to look deeper into Tessara. Don't you think that warrants a look?"

"He said that before Isaacs took down Winslow. Trust me, that was the only connection. You don't get government contracts without being thoroughly vet-ted. Tessara is clean."

He didn't believe it. Miko wouldn't have said that if that were the case. "I'd like to poke around Tes-sara, but first I want to talk to Nathan again and see if he left anything out of his statement."

"Such as?" Jane asked, frowning. "Are you saying that Isaacs could've withheld evidence?"

"No. But maybe he forgot some details. It's not as if Nathan didn't get caught up in some hairy shit, too. Winslow almost won that fight. Nathan was in ICU for weeks recovering from a bullet wound to the gut, and that's no cakewalk."

"I read the file. Even bleeding out, he managed to take a beating from Winslow before killing her. Impressive," she admitted. "Nathan Isaacs is a bit of a badass."

Yeah, it was true. He wouldn't steal Nathan's thun-der just because the sudden admirable light in Jane's eyes caused a spurt of jealousy from out of nowhere. So instead, he said, "He's a good man. One of the best."

Jane nodded, and it was apparent he'd caused the

wheels to start moving, which was a good thing. He'd rather have her working with him than against. "Fine, we can talk to Isaacs, but everything is going on the record. I don't want anyone using the excuse they won't talk unless they have anonymity."

"Sometimes you have to bend the rules, Fallon," he told her, giving her no such promise. When lives were at stake, sometimes regs went out the window. He'd do whatever it took to get the real answers, and that included twisting the rules into a pretzel.

"You're impossible to work with," she groused under her breath as they walked into the main room. The bar was off to the right, and a pool table stood, dejected and forgotten, on the left. Jane noticed the table and said, "I'm surprised they didn't immediately sell that at auction."

"Me, too," he said, frowning. Everything of value had been stripped from the bar, including Miko's collectible tap handles he'd purchased for a steal on eBay. Holden strode to the pool table and ran his palm over the familiar green felt. He and Miko had played many games on this table and wagered more money than they should've because they were both so damn competitive. A smile tugged at his mouth at the memory. "Miko was a terrible pool player but a great cheater. I wouldn't be surprised if he'd found a way to slant the table to his advantage. He didn't even deny the fact he didn't play fair. The sucker was always taking me for a couple hundred every time we played."

"So much for that honor you were talking about," she quipped drily, and Holden shook his head.

"No, it wasn't like that. He considered any *competition* fair game. Second place is first loser. C'mon, Fallon, you can't tell me you don't feel the same."

"True," she agreed grudgingly. "But I don't condone cheating of any kind. If you can't win on your own merits, you don't deserve to win."

He grunted a concession and bent down to inspect the ball return. "Maybe it's broken and they figured whoever bought the place could either throw it away or have it repaired." He felt along the track. The balls gleamed in the dim light, a reminder of better times. He pulled three quarters from his pocket and slid them into the coin return, pushing it in, but the coins slid back out, answering that question. "Yeah, it's broken," he said, reaching underneath to feel along the underside. The pads of his fingers found a tiny button and he stopped, motioning for Jane to bring the light. "I feel something…a button of some sort. I don't know much about pool tables, but I can't imagine why there'd be a button underneath the table." Jane came closer and bent to peer beneath the table with the light. "You see anything?"

"That's odd," she agreed. "Press it and see what happens."

"Famous last words," Holden quipped with a grin and she grimaced at his humor. But soon neither were laughing because suddenly a hidden door released and a taped manila envelope dropped to the floor. "What the… Miko, you crafty son of a bitch…"

"What the hell is that?" Jane asked, the cold forgotten and her eyes trained on the envelope. "Why would your brother hide something in the pool table?"

"Because no one would think to look there," he answered with pride for his brother's smarts. "Good one, bro."

"That's evidence," she said, moving to stop him before he ripped open the package. "We should give it to the forensics team and let them determine what's inside."

"Screw that. My brother put it there. I'm sure of it."

"How can you be so sure?"

"Because of the way it's taped. Miko always wrapped envelopes with three strips of tape with a crisscross at the back so he'd know if anyone else tried to read his mail and then reseal it."

"Weird...but okay. We should still give it to forensics."

"Whatever is in this envelope is not leaving my hot little hands." He tucked the envelope into the interior pocket of his jacket, and after one final sweep of the bar, he headed for the door, satisfied they'd found all that would be of use to them there. "Let's go before we turn into popsicles."

"You're seriously not going to turn that envelope over to the proper authorities?"

"Nope. As far as I'm concerned, the proper authorities haven't done a good enough job to earn my trust with this case. And that definitely includes you."

She glared, but he didn't care. "You make it really hard to like you," she finally said.

He grinned. "That's okay, honey. I ain't looking for

a dinner date. C'mon, let's go someplace secure and see what my brother kept squirreled away."

His hands were frozen, but his heart was lighter than it'd been in months. Finally, a break. Thank God for Miko's penchant for hiding things. It was oddly comforting to know that even though Miko had changed, some things had remained the same.

Chapter 6

Jane remained silent once they'd climbed into the car. She'd been absolutely certain she'd missed nothing in her investigation, but the second Holden had discovered that hidden manila envelope, everything she'd thought she'd known came into question. Was there more to this case than she'd originally thought? And if so, what did that mean? Who was involved? It hurt her head to think the corruption centered at I.D. was bigger than they could imagine. "How had you known to keep looking?" she asked, breaking the silence. "As far as I could tell, we were staring at an empty building. But you sensed there was something hidden. How?"

Holden shrugged, as if he really didn't know and his inability to put it into words made him uncomfortable. "I guess it's the twin thing. Miko and I shared a bond. And I just knew I was missing something. It's like an itch you can't scratch, except that it's at the back of your mind, nagging, whining in your ear." He stopped as if he hadn't liked the way his explanation had come out and finished with another shrug, saying, "I don't know. I just knew."

"Why would Miko hide something in the pool table?" she asked, mostly to herself. "I have to be honest, the discovery of that envelope opens up a whole other realm of questions that I'm not entirely comfortable with."

"I can imagine."

"Oh? Can you?" She didn't try to hide the bitterness in her voice. Her father was not going to be happy about this newest development. "Obviously he didn't want anyone to find it. And if he didn't tell you about it, something in that envelope must be important."

"My thoughts, too. Which is why we're not taking it back to the office," he said, surprising her. He cut her a short look just as she started to protest. "Listen, I don't know how far or how deep the corruption went with I.D., but I do know that my brother got caught up in something bad. So forgive me if I'm not too trusting right now."

"Even with your own team?"

"It's nothing personal, but I can't afford mistakes. My brother died. Yes, he may have pulled the trigger, but someone else was pulling the strings. You know what I mean?"

"That's one theory," she reminded him, not quite on board yet that Miko hadn't been pulling the wool over everyone's eyes, including his brother's. "The other theory is that Miko had plenty to hide because he was doing things he knew were wrong."

"Miko was the soldier, more so than I ever was. He believed in doing the right thing and standing up for the little guy who couldn't stand up for himself. He had integrity, grit, a singular sense of justice," Holden said, holding his ground, obviously determined to defend his brother to anyone and everyone. "And I refuse to believe that in one year's time he became the polar opposite of everything he ever held true."

"People change," she said, trying to soften the harsh truth. "And sometimes we don't even know what happened."

"I'm going to find who's pulling the strings. I don't care how long it takes or what it costs me. And when I find him or her...I want to put that person into the ground."

She suppressed a shudder at the menace in Holden's voice. A part of her wanted to remind him this was the reason he hadn't been allowed to investigate the case in the first place. Emotional attachments muddied a person's ability to think rationally. But there was another part of her, the part that admired his loyalty and tenacity, that couldn't deny the sharp pull of attraction. He was damn sexy when he was going all *Rambo* and *Rebel Without a Cause,* even if it was the most reckless attitude she'd ever witnessed. She swallowed and cleared her voice, not liking the way her thoughts were tumbling through her head. "And just where do you plan to take this evidence?"

"Back to my place."

"It's evidence and needs to be logged properly," she maintained stubbornly. "You're dangerously close to going rogue. Don't screw your career trying to avenge your brother."

"I'm not killing my career. I'm chasing leads. You already had a chance to dig deep into this case. You were content to look at the surface, and that's just not the case with me. When I'm done learning whatever I can from the contents of the envelope, I will log it properly. Until then, it's not leaving my side."

She could tell it was no use arguing with him on this point. She'd been around enough stubborn men to know when the smartest course of action was to back down and try a different tact. *Motto for the day: Fight smart.* "Fine. But I'm coming with you. I need to make sure the integrity of the case remains unsullied, even if you are using unorthodox methods. And that point is nonnegotiable."

Holden probably didn't like her terms, but he didn't shoot them down, either. Holden was a lot of things—stupid wasn't one of them. At least they had that in their favor.

Soon enough, they arrived at Holden's apartment, and Jane had to tamp down the mild flutters erupting in her belly at the memories surfacing. She could chastise herself all day for allowing her thoughts to wander, but she enjoyed the seductive allure that came with lingering over that brief time in her life. She couldn't lie—they'd enjoyed some good times. "Did it ever occur to you when you were apartment shopping to consider a place that didn't look like a prison from the outside?" she asked with a healthy dose of sarcasm, and he responded with a grunt. Such a Chatty Cathy, she wanted to grumble. Would it kill him to engage just a little? She followed him through the gated entrance and then up the long flight of stairs to his door. From the outside, the nondescript gray building was nothing to look at, and since everything was covered in snow, not a hint of foliage was visible, either. "Not much for ambiance," she said under her breath, to which Holden just kept walking.

"I'm not interested in making the place look inviting. The less traffic, the better."

"Such the people person," she said, walking into his spacious apartment. The first time she'd seen his place, her jaw had dropped to the floor. Never in a million years would she have imagined such an awesome bachelor pad tucked in this building. It was like something featured in *Architectural Digest,* with its high ceilings and polished bamboo flooring, and the decor was tastefully masculine without appearing to lack a woman's touch. Holden had knocked down the walls connected to three more apartments, which heightened the chic appearance and immediately told people that this wasn't your average apartment. And seeing it again, not just through the sliver of an open door like the other night when she'd visited him, was enough to fill her with awe all over again.

"God, I'd forgotten how much I covet your apartment," she blurted.

The tiniest quirk of a smile was his only response as he tossed his keys into a small ceramic bowl by the door. He went straight to the gleaming kitchen and grabbed a bottled water from the stainless steel refrigerator and tossed another to her. "Sorry, but it's a package deal. Can't have the apartment without me," he said with a shrug. "And you've already kicked me to the curb."

Why'd he have to constantly bring up their past? It was getting old. She turned to face him. "Can you stop being a whiny baby for two minutes? I can't believe how petulant you sound."

"You're right," he said, grinning. "Can't seem to help myself when you're around. Low-hanging fruit and all that."

"Well, try," she told him and opened the water bottle. "Here's something I've always wondered…how did you manage to convince the owner to give you three apartments so you could make these changes?"

"I own the building. As long as I got the right permits, the city let me do whatever I want."

"You own the building?"

"Yeah? Didn't I mention that before?"

"No."

He chuckled as if it were no big deal and said, "Well, now you know. I own the building. It's the best way to control who your neighbors are."

Wasn't that the truth. If she'd been in charge of her apartment complex, she never would've allowed dogs.

Her immediate neighbor had a small, yappy purse dog that barked at all hours of the night. Before Jane had invested in earplugs, she'd wanted to commit a crime that PETA would've persecuted her for. She'd even gone so far as to measure the width of the trash chute and, yep, a small dog would totally fit through the opening. "I suppose so," she admitted with a shrug before slanting a curious gaze at him. "And *how* exactly did you afford this building?"

"Smart investments. I bought it years ago when housing values were still manageable. Cosmetically, it was in bad shape, but the bones were good, so I did the work myself, with some help from Miko when he could manage it. Once we were finished, I was judicious about who I rented to. All in all, it's worked out pretty well."

She whistled with appreciation. "I should say so. Holden, I never thought I'd say this about anything involving you, but I'm jealous."

"I don't blame you. Your apartment sucks."

Her cheeks heated and she wrinkled her nose at him. "Yeah, well, not everyone is independently wealthy, as you apparently are."

"Not wealthy, I just have an eye for good investments."

"I guess so. A bachelor pad like this probably bags plenty of chicks. I imagine the hardest part is getting them to leave."

"I suppose it could be, but I don't bring chicks here."

She tried not to let his admission floor her. Had

she been the only woman he'd brought here? She'd thought for sure he'd use this place to get plenty of tail. "Really? So all of this grand architecture and stylish decor is just for your benefit?"

"Pretty much. Your home should be your sanctuary. When I come home, I don't want other people crowding my space. You know what I mean? When I walk through my front door, I try to leave everything else behind. And if I started bringing chicks here, it would change the energy of the place. Plus, I don't like women knowing where I live. It gets messy."

"So why'd you bring me here?" She shouldn't have asked, but she had and there was no taking it back.

His gaze darkened. "Do you really want to know the answer to that?"

She swallowed. Maybe not. She nodded anyway. "Yeah."

"Because you were special. I know you don't believe me, but I don't go around telling women that I love them unless I mean it."

A strange, sizzling burn skidded across her chest, and she had to suck back the gasp from the unexpected pain. Why did he have to go throwing the *L* word around? It wasn't that she didn't believe him or she hadn't felt something in return, but she'd known that if she didn't end things, it would've ended messily later. "Well, I guess that's ancient history," she returned briskly, forcing a smile. "I think we both dodged a bullet. I don't think either one of us is cut out for the *until death do us part* thing. It would've been a nightmare in the end."

"I guess we'll never know." A shadow passed over his face and she suffered the knowledge that she'd hurt him, probably more so than she'd realized at the time. However, as evidenced by the way her dad had reacted to Holden's little sit-down-and-chat, she really had saved him years of misery. "And now the conversation just got too angsty," he announced, breaking the silence between them as he pulled the envelope from his satchel. "Let's put a pin in all that 'ancient history,' as you call it and see what's in this envelope," he suggested, redirecting. He had a point— they weren't here to gab like girlfriends; they were here to open that envelope. Jane took a long drink of water as Holden used his Leatherman pocket knife to slice open the envelope. He dumped the contents carefully onto his granite countertop.

"Wow, someone was saving for a rainy day," she observed as money, at least twenty thousand dollars, dropped to the counter along with several passports and driver's licenses. Jane grabbed the first passport closest to her. "This isn't your brother's name," she said, showing Holden the fake ID. "None of these are. Why would he need multiple aliases?"

He frowned. "I don't know." Holden pushed the cash out of the way and grabbed the IDs. "Three different identities, none of which I've ever heard of." He read the addresses. "Mexico, Switzerland, London. What were you into, Miko?" he muttered. "What the hell were you doing?"

Wasn't it painfully obvious? "Holden, he was getting ready to run because he knew he'd been caught.

For whatever reason, he decided to kill himself instead." Jane would have to be the bad guy. She tacked on, "I'm sorry," because she did feel the tiniest bit of regret that she'd been right all along. She wasn't an ogre. Holden had obviously loved his brother. "Give it some time," she suggested. "With some distance… you'll start to feel better."

Holden shook his head, that stubborn look returning to his expression. "No, my brother would never leave me behind. You can argue all you want, but I know he wouldn't. It's that twin thing I told you about earlier."

She smothered a sound of frustration. "How many more clues do you need that prove your brother was guilty?" she asked. "Look, I know how hard this must be. And honestly, I was kind of hoping we might find a different answer, but the facts seem pretty clear."

His dark chuckle made her groan. Holden braced himself on the counter, leaning toward her. "They're clear, are they? I'm sure they're *very* clear for you. We both know this investigation is not high on your priority list. I know how this looks for you. I'm not stupid. And I know I'm asking a lot for you to trust me, and sometimes we don't even like each other, but when I tell you there's more to this story, you're just going to have to believe me and help me get to the bottom of this."

"Why? Like you said, tearing apart my own investigation isn't high on my to-do list."

"Because your type A brain won't let the possibility that you screwed up pass you by. It'll eat at you until you find the answers, even if you don't like the answers you find."

He knew her pretty well. She'd like to say it was because working in the same office, rubbing shoulders—wanted or not—would do that if paired with an observant person, but Holden knew her in a way she wanted to forget because it hurt to remember. Of course, she couldn't let him know that. "Your point?" she shot back.

"My point is you know if you push past the obvious, you'll see what I see. There's more to this story than we've been told. And you want to get to the bottom of it."

"Yeah? Why?"

"Do I have to spell it out?"

"No," she allowed with a sigh, hating he had her figured out when he was constantly surprising her. "If it turns out you're right, cracking open the true case will look good for my résumé and help give you closure about your brother. I get it!" Jane glared, hating he was right. "I said I'd give you the week. My word is good. But we better find more than just an envelope full of cash and some fake IDs as your proof Miko wasn't a traitor."

"A week is all I'm asking for."

She was taking a big risk with Holden. It felt as if she were standing on the edge of a really big fall—and Holden was the one leading her straight to the cliff.

Chapter 7

Holden stared at the IDs Miko had stashed in the pool table. London, Switzerland, Mexico—all three places were common refuges for people who wanted to disappear. He lined the IDs in a row on the counter, letting his brain work through the tangle of questions. Next his focus moved to the cash. Twenty thousand was a lot of money, but it wasn't enough to live off of for long, which meant Miko likely had money stashed elsewhere. How to find the money was the question. He couldn't go through his usual channels; he had to go underground. He knew of a guy—through his friend Nathan Isaacs—but it wasn't a strong connection. And frankly, the guy had nearly got killed the last time he had helped out on a high-stakes mission. The memory of that mission was enough to make

Holden shake his head with a dark chuckle. Most people would freak out if they knew the kind of games the government played with everyday lives. Just ask Jake Isaacs, Nathan's younger brother, who was still recovering from a dose of MCX-209, an experimental drug that'd temporarily wiped out his memories. The drug should've been destroyed and all of the research on it thrown into an incinerator, but everything pertaining to MCX-209 was under the lock and key of the Defense Intelligence Agency—including the doctor who'd created the drug, Dr. Kat Odgers. But as much as Holden didn't want to involve another civilian, he didn't see another choice. He called up his friend Nathan and hoped for the best.

"Hey, Holden, everything okay?" Nathan said as soon as he answered. In spite of the three-hour time difference, Nathan didn't sound sleepy. Insomnia was something most vets came home with, and Nathan was no different. Miko and Nathan had been tight, serving in the same unit and later working for I.D. as snipers. They'd shared a bond, similar to what Holden and Miko had shared, and Holden trusted Nathan. "I heard about the decision to strip Miko of his honors. That's rough, man. Just know that Miko was not the sum of his medals but the integrity of his heart. Keep that close and it doesn't matter what the Powers That Be take from him."

Holden closed his eyes, riding out the sting. "Thanks, man. But that's not why I'm calling."

"No? What's up?"

"I have a real small window to prove that Miko didn't do the things he's been accused of."

"Really? How did you manage that?"

"Luck and being as stubborn as a mule. But listen, this is what I need your help with—do you still have contact information for that computer guy? You know the one that made the virus that disabled the Zephyr system at the compound?"

"James Cotton? Yeah, I have his digits. But Jaci will have a fit if she finds out we're dragging her friend back into danger. She stresses over all this 'spy stuff,' as she calls it."

Jaci and Nathan had certainly been through the ringer together during the I.D. investigation. Aside from Nathan almost dying, a thug had broken Jaci's finger in order to prove a point to Nathan. At the time, Jaci had been lucky only her finger had been broken—it could've been so much worse.

"I don't blame her. People die and sometimes there's no answers when they get involved with fringe government. All I can do is make my case. The guy will either say yes or he'll say no, right?"

"True enough. Chances are James will say yes because he lives for a challenge, and for all his smarts doesn't seem to have the good sense God gave a goose. Can you tell me what's going on?"

"I'm not sure what there is to tell, but I found three IDs and passports in a hidden location and I need to know if Miko was stashing money in other countries. The only way to find that out is to go through backdoor channels. I'm assuming your guy can do that, right?"

"James can do things that are so highly illegal I don't even know how he's still walking the streets."

Holden laughed. "Excellent. That's just the kind of guy I need."

"In all seriousness, do you really think you have some solid evidence that could save Miko's reputation?"

Holden heard the hope in Nathan's voice and he understood that yearning because he felt it, too. "I sure as hell hope so. It's weak, but it's all I have to go on. I just have this feeling that if I chase it down, I'll be able to find what I'm looking for."

"Is there anything I can do to help?"

"Not just yet. I don't want to drag you into this. You've been through enough."

"It's all in the past. Nothing but good things to look forward to now. You know, you might give Jake and his girl a call. They are up in Washington, too, doing that top-secret defense intelligence stuff. They might be able to open some doors for you that otherwise might stay closed. That is, if things with James don't work out."

"I appreciate it, man. How's Jake feeling?"

"He's not one hundred percent, but he's doing damn good considering what he went through. He still has gaps in his memory. He's getting better, though. He might even recover fully. Unfortunately, only time will tell."

"That drug was scary shit. I wish they would've

just dropped all the research into the ocean. Or down a deep, dark hole. That kind of stuff shouldn't be in anyone's hands. Not even our government's."

"Amen, brother."

Holden thanked Nathan and ended the call. A few moments later, his phone chirped with the contact information he needed. He logged the name into his phone and then called Cotton, aka Ghost.

"Yeah?" James answered. "Who's this?"

"Hey, James, not sure if you remember me, but my name's Holden Archangelo—"

"Yeah, I remember you. Your brother, Miko, used to run with Nathan Isaacs."

"You have a good memory."

"Comes with being a genius. I'm assuming this isn't a call to go get drinks or something. What do you need hacked?"

He appreciated the man's straightforward attack. Holden wasn't interested in chitchat either, so he got right to the point. "I need you to trace some money. My brother may have stashed cash in three different countries and I need to know why and how much."

"You're government grade, so why don't you do it yourself?" he asked, then added, "Unless you can't because you're doing this on the down low."

"Bingo. Think you can handle this?"

"Oh, I have no doubt I can handle it. The real question is, should I? The last time I had a play date with you cats, I nearly got my balls shot off and frankly, I'm fairly attached to that part of my anatomy."

"Fair enough. I can't guarantee your safety, and there's a chance my brother was hiding from seriously bad people. However, something tells me you can't help but hunger for a challenge."

"Nice pitch. So what I'm hearing is danger, high level of threat and virtually zero benefit for me aside from the street cred in my personal circles. I don't know, maybe I'm getting old, but that's not enough."

"You drive a hard bargain."

"Or maybe I just wised up."

"What's it going to take, then?"

"Well, my car got blown up the last go around and I'm still taking the bus."

"You want me to buy you a car?" Holden asked, incredulous at the guy's nerve.

"Seems only fair."

"The Isaacs brothers ought to be the ones buying you a car. That was their op that got your ride blown to bits."

"Yeah, well, Jaci is my best friend and that just seems wrong to demand that from her and her husband, and Jake, well, he's not quite right in the head, so how nice would it look if I was shaking down a guy with special needs?"

"Jake is hardly special needs. The guy could take you out with his bare hands and a piece of twine."

"MacGyver style, I get it. Still, doesn't seem right. Besides, they don't need my help—you do. And to be honest, I don't even know you, so why should I risk my neck for a stranger?"

Valid points. "All right. How about twenty grand? That ought to be enough scratch to buy you a car."

"Twenty Gs? Yeah, that'll work," he said, whistling. "I accept your offer. Wire the cash and then I'll contact you."

"Look at you, all eager and shit. No," he said, countering firmly. "Here's how it's going down. I will wire half of the cash now and half on delivery of the information. Got it?"

"I respect that. You have a deal."

Holden gave a minute shake of his head, silently laughing at the guy's tough-guy routine when he knew for a fact James Cotton was no marine. But hey, Holden respected his grab for some personal gain. People had to eat. "Expect the wire by the end of the day. And then I expect results within forty-eight hours. Got it?"

"Forty-eight hours? I'm not a magician."

"Well, if you want to be paid, you ought to start learning some new tricks."

"You government types are all the same—expecting the delivery of the moon and then demanding it within an impossible time frame."

"Hey, forty-eight was generous. My original offer was going to be twenty-four." At that he clicked off, smirking. From what he knew of James, the guy had an ego. With any luck, he'd beat that deadline with time to spare just so he could gloat. And that was fine by Holden. He wanted—no, he *needed*—answers now.

* * *

Jane sipped her wine and settled into the bathtub, giving in to a rare luxury. She never indulged in such a girlie thing, but her muscles ached and her brain was cluttered, and she was just ready to chill out for once.

Steam heated the room into a humid sauna. She didn't mind. She liked the heat. Living in Washington, she suffered through the horrid winters just so she could get to the humid summers. Maybe someday she'd move to Florida. No, scratch that—she didn't like alligators. Maybe Georgia or some other place in the South. She liked to fantasize about leaving D.C., but in truth, she knew she wasn't going anywhere. Her home was here, where she was firmly rooted. Her father and brothers would have a fit if she tried to move. She was the one who took care of the mundane details of their father's life, and neither of her brothers were going to take on that job. Nope. As her father liked to drill into his kids, everyone had a detail, a task, and only weaklings and pathetic losers shirked their responsibilities onto others. Like her mother.

Jane took a bigger sip of the wine, bordering on a gulp, and tried not to think of her mother, but sometimes, in spite of her best efforts, a memory or two squeaked by her defenses.

It'd been a sunny day in August when The Major had sat all three of his children on the sofa, requiring their undivided attention as he shared the intel of their mother abandoning them.

"It has come to my attention that your mother has gone AWOL from this family unit," he'd said gruffly, clasping both hands behind his back and pacing a short line before them. "This is both an unexpected and disappointing turn of events, but it's nothing we can't handle."

Faced with two stoic brothers who'd turned to stone the moment their father had shared the news, she'd had little choice but to keep a stiff upper lip, also. The Major didn't tolerate crybabies. Each of the Fallon children was expected to pick up the slack their defecting mother had created, and it didn't matter they were young and confused as to why their mother would suddenly abandon them. It was soldier on or get left behind.

Jane had taken on the house details—including cooking, shopping and paying the bills. Walker and Ian were in charge of everything related to the outside and repair work. They were a well-oiled machine.

Without a shred of emotion allowed.

Their mother had made contact once, but Jane had been too desperate for her father's love to accept her mom's attempt at reaching out. She winced at the memory....

"Janie," her mother had said. "I'm settled now. I know the boys would probably rather stay with their father but...perhaps you'd like to come and stay with me?"

"And why would I want to do that?" Jane had asked in a voice colder than any twelve-year-old should be able to muster. "You abandoned us all a year ago and now you want to act like you're a mother? Too little, too late."

"Janie!" her mother had admonished her in an anguished tone. "Why are you so cold to me? Let me explain…there are some things that a child simply can't understand."

"I understand that you left. What else is there?"

Her mother had skipped answering the question and tried a different tactic, almost desperately. "Sweetie…you're reaching an age when a girl needs her mother. Surely, you realize your father is ill equipped to handle the needs of a young girl."

She had realized that. The mere mention of bra shopping had been excruciating for them both. In the end, The Major had simply thrown a wad of cash in her direction and with reddened cheeks had instructed her to purchase whatever was necessary. Of course, Jane hadn't had a clue and ended up with a bra two sizes too small. It'd felt like wearing a corset. But she wasn't about to concede any weakness to the enemy, her mother. "Not necessary," she'd said. "I can care for myself."

"I could go to court and compel you to come stay with me," she'd said. "But I won't do that. If you don't want to be with me, I won't force you."

But a secret part of her had hoped her mother would do exactly that so she didn't have a choice in the matter. Surely, her father couldn't blame her if the court had stepped in. And she missed her mother. In her darkest, deepest, most shamefully weak part of herself…she wished her mother hadn't left. But that hadn't been her reality and she'd dealt with it. Her mother had tried a few more times, but Jane had finally stopped taking her calls and then, as expected, her mother had finally stopped phoning.

Jane swirled her wine. How would things have been different if her mother had stuck it out? Maybe if The Major hadn't been so rigid...well, that was like wishing the tide would stop licking the shore. As long as there was a moon, there would be a tide. Some things would never change.

Including her father.

Stop this melancholy over a past long gone, she chastised herself, banishing the memories. But apparently her brain was up to playing games because as soon as her thoughts cleared of family drama, she thought of Holden. The alcohol loosened her grip on what was appropriate, and she immediately mused on how perfect Holden's physique was and how, maybe, in an alternate universe, they could've stayed together.

She missed quiet evenings spent curled on his sofa, watching eighties movies and arguing over what constituted a cult classic. The memory of one particular night made her sigh.

"*The Breakfast Club* is vastly superior to *Top Gun,*" she'd protested, throwing popcorn at him when he'd refused to budge. "We're talking archetypal characters that completely capture the angst and uncertainty of being a teenager, all with a kick-ass soundtrack and the best dialogue ever written. There's no way a movie about the navy's cocky fly-bys is better."

Holden grinned as if he had the ace. "Anything with fighter jets in the movie automatically ratchets the score a few points, which, of course, buries your movie about a bunch of whiny teenagers bitching about spending an afternoon together."

"But don't you get it? It's an entire movie spent picking apart the daily lives of the American teen, showing in excruciating detail the pressures teens face in modern society."

Holden had rolled his eyes and faked a yawn, then added, "Fighter pilots. And a kick-ass soundtrack—not to mention—" he paused for effect "—Kelly Mc-Gillis. She's hot for an old lady."

"Really? You're such a man."

"Yes, I am," he had agreed with a shameless grin as he pulled her on top of him. She'd laughed and fallen against his chest, knocking popcorn everywhere. "You can concede defeat and I'll accept your surrender."

"Who says I'm surrendering?" She had looped her arms around his neck and pulled him close so their lips touched. After a long, deep kiss, she'd smiled against his mouth and said, "This feels like victory to me...."

"No fair using your womanly wiles. I have no defense against them."

"I know." She had laughed. "Now admit that my movie is better than yours."

"Never."

She'd nibbled his neck and nipped his ear, sweetening the deal. "Concede and I'll let you do whatever you want with me."

He had sucked in a sharp breath and rose up, wild excitement darkening his gaze. "Anything?"

"Anything," she'd promised in a sultry whisper.

"You win! I concede! *The Breakfast Club* rules." And then he'd hopped off and pulled her to her feet to scoop her up in his arms. "You, my dear, may find victory exhausting."

Holden had spent the rest of the night pleasuring Jane in ways that had to be illegal in some places, leaving her in a state of total sated lethargy that'd seeped into the following day at the office. The sizzling memory made it hard to focus on work and each time they invariably ran into each other, she hadn't been able to meet Holden's gaze without blushing and trying to hide the all-over body tingle that shivered over her skin. Oh, yeah, Holden had definitely won that round, even if he'd admitted defeat.

Jane's legs moved restlessly beneath the water, and she finished her wine with a quick swallow. What was she doing reminiscing about Holden? To what end? Total mortification, humiliation and endless mockery if he ever found out? Ugh. She rose from her bath and grabbed her towel. Enough tub time. She needed her head on straight if she was going to remain shoulder to shoulder with Archangelo. This girlie stuff was enough to give her the heebie-jeebies.

This ridiculous attraction to Holden could go right where she stored her feelings about her mother— tucked away in subzero.

Chapter 8

The following day, Reed called them both into his office first thing. The permanent frown marks etched into their boss's face seemed a bit deeper this morning, which meant he wasn't about to ask them if they were interested in purchasing Girl Scout cookies from his granddaughter. "Shut the door and take a seat," he directed, motioning to them both. "You know I'm not a fan of conspiracy theories, but something's not right about this case. Yesterday I got a visit from someone associated with Tessara Pharm with information that he shouldn't have had. *Classified* information. The whole conversation gave me a bad vibe, and frankly, pissed me off because the guy's attitude stank of arrogance."

"What kind of questions was he asking?" Jane

asked. "And how do you think he came by the information?"

"He was mostly asking about the investigation and why it had been reopened. The fact that he knew there was action on the case gave me a bad feeling. *No one* should know that you two are looking into new evidence. It seems Tessara Pharm has people with a long-armed reach."

"Nothing like finding out that classified information isn't as secure as you think," Jane said, concerned.

"Yeah, exactly. So what do you have so far?"

Holden shared a look with Jane, not entirely ready to share what they'd found, though it seemed he'd have to give Reed something. "We went back to my brother's bar and we found something that may have some significance, but it's too early to tell. We're in the process of chasing it down."

"Such as?" Reed gestured with impatience. "Don't make me drag it out of you. Just spit it out."

Jane jumped in, surprising Holden. "Sir, if I may, it's sensitive, and given the fact that information is being leaked to people outside of classified channels, Holden and I would rather keep our evidence close to the breast for the time being."

"All right." Reed grunted in understanding even if he didn't like it. "I'll give you that. I don't know how Ulysses Rocha came across the information that he did, but you're right in that our usual channels don't seem secure. Just answer me this—do you think there's something to your suspicion that Miko was involved in something bigger?"

Holden nodded gravely. "I do. I think the fact that Tessara Pharm is poking around in our investigation lends further credence to that belief."

Jane's nod betrayed none of her own misgivings. Holden owed her one. He knew that her word was solid. If she said she'd give him a week, a week he'd get and not a minute more or less. That was all he could ask for. "I think our next step should be to make a stop in at Tessara Pharm, don't you?"

"That's a long flight for a conversation," Reed groused. "What's wrong with the phone?"

"Gotta see the whites of their eyes, sir," Jane answered and Holden agreed. "Microexpressions, body language—those things you can't pick up on the phone."

"All right. I'll approve the expenditure, only because that Ulysses guy rubbed me wrong. But keep it short and sweet and don't go ruffling feathers. I don't want even more eyes on us during this investigation. This needs to be done by the numbers and without prejudice. Got it?"

Holden smiled. "Of course."

"Stow that shit-eating grin, Archangelo. Don't think for a second I don't regret letting you poke around in a closed case. I have a feeling this is going to earn more than just extra paperwork. I have a headache already."

Holden smothered his smile under an appropriately stern look of gratitude to his superior. "Yes, sir," he said, and followed Jane out of Harris's office and headed to their desks. Once in their respective seats, Jane booked plane reservations while he prepared to call Nathan. "Since we're going to be in California, we might as well hit up Nathan, too. I have some questions regarding the last time he saw my brother alive."

"You sure you want to do that?" Jane asked. "It's not a pretty story."

"I know. I've read your report. But Nathan might tell me a few things that weren't in the report."

Jane stiffened. "You mean you think he might've deliberately withheld information?"

"Calm down, G.I. Jane," he said drily. "Nathan and Miko were buds, that's all. They knew each other as friends, not just as peers. Maybe all we'll do is share a beer and swap stories. Or maybe he'll have something important to share." He gestured to the airline page on her computer, adding, "Oh, and make sure it's first class...I need the legroom."

Jane rolled her eyes and turned to her computer to book the reservations.

Determined to make good use of her time during the flight, Jane took out her notebook the moment they were buckled in and ascending. It was eight hours to California, and she didn't want to waste valuable time. "So let's go over what we know so far," she suggested, taking a second to appreciate the first-class accommodations. Holden was right—there *was* more legroom. "I figure it's a good idea to consolidate the facts before we land so we know exactly what we're doing and who we're going to be talking to when we get there."

A spark of appreciation lit up Holden's gaze, and she tried not to read more into it than the moment warranted. But even as he seemed to like her initiative, it seemed Holden wasn't about to discuss the case on the plane. "Your enthusiasm is admirable, but I don't feel comfortable talking about the case here. Too many ears."

Jane glanced around the first-class cabin. Although the odds were slim that anyone there might compromise their investigation, she sighed and tucked her notebook away because that 1 percent chance wouldn't let her insist. "I guess I could take a nap, then," she said, disappointed. She couldn't help but add, "For the record, I think you're being a little paranoid."

"Haven't you ever watched a spy movie? The person you overlook is always the one you should watch out for."

"I don't base my life around the flimsy plots of action movies."

"Flimsy? You've obviously never watched any of the Bourne movies. And this is coming from the same woman who once argued pretty convincingly about the merits of an eighties John Hughes movie?"

Her cheeks flushed at the casual reference of that night, and she shot him a quelling look. He dropped the jocularity to say, "I'm not discussing this case unless we're alone. Sorry, but the stakes are just too high for me to take the chance, no matter how slim the odds are that someone might be listening."

She supposed if one of her brothers' reputations was on the line, she wouldn't take any unnecessary risks, either. "I see your point," she conceded with an unhappy sigh. She could always take that nap. She ought to be tired because she hadn't slept well last night, but her eyes weren't about to close, not when she was wedged this close to Holden. She didn't trust what she might mumble in her sleep, given her recent private musings. Unsettled, she shifted away from Holden as much as the seat would allow. He caught the motion and called her on it. "Do you think I have cooties or something? I promise I do bathe regularly. I even brush my teeth on occasion." To illustrate, he flashed his pearly whites.

"It has nothing to do with you," she lied. "I just like my personal space. And I hate flying," she muttered, silencing him by adding tersely, "And don't try to lecture me that flying is safer than driving. I *know* the statistics. It's a mental thing, so just leave me be about it."

Holden seemed vastly amused by her admission, his grin widening. "You're afraid of flying?"

She bristled. "I didn't say I was *afraid*. I just said I don't like it. If God meant for us to fly, he would've given us wings."

Holden laughed. "Who knew that tough-as-nails Jane Fallon was afraid of a little modern technology?"

"I'm not afraid of modern technology," she insisted. "I love my smartphone. Just something about the idea of flying doesn't sit right in my head. I mean think about it…how are we even staying up in the air? No, don't answer. I know the physics. I'm simply saying fundamentally this giant cargo bus should not be flying around like a huge bumblebee in the sky."

"Just when I think I have you figured out—you go and say something that completely tips what I think I know on its head."

Holden thought he had her figured out? That would be the day. But she was a tiny bit flattered that he'd tried. "Don't get too comfortable, Archangelo. I'm a person you would never be able to figure out."

"When you say that, I hear a challenge. And I can't in good conscience let a challenge go without answering the siren call."

"Oh, is that so?" She tried not to find his smirk adorable, but it was doing weird things to her stomach. She bumped him with her shoulder like she would any ol' dude. "Talk about testosterone overload." Were all guys the same? Or maybe it was all guys in the military. Her brothers were the same way. And her father. "Let's put a pin in your curiosity about me and share something about Miko, maybe about growing up together."

Holden relaxed and a small smile formed on his lips, though she saw the ghost of grief hovering around the edges. "What do you want to know?"

"I don't know. What was he like as a kid? Was he like you?"

"People assume because we were twins we were

exact copies of one another, but really, we were nothing alike."

"How so?"

"For one, Miko was a better man than me."

That shocked her. "Why would you say that?"

"Because it's the truth. Miko was ruled by an intense need for justice. That's why he went into the military, whereas I went because I wanted someone to pay for my college. But Miko wanted to do something for the greater good. He took pride in the fact that he did what others couldn't. He was always one for the underdog."

"So how do you think he got involved with Tessara and Penny Winslow?" she asked, frowning against the information she knew from her investigation and the man Holden was championing. It almost seemed as if they were two different people. "It appears that Tessara got under his skin in a bad way."

He nodded, just as baffled. "That's the question that keeps me up at night. Everything I know about Miko doesn't jibe with the facts as they've been played out. He didn't care about money or material things, but that's exactly how that report paints him to be. A mercenary is all about the money, and that's the opposite of Miko. Yeah, he made good change with I.D.—no doubt about it—but it wasn't what he cared about. Others might be about the paycheck. However, for Miko, it was something different. I know he felt he was doing something for his country that no one else could." He sighed. "Somewhere along the way, things got tangled."

"Do you think at some point he realized he was in over his head?"

"Definitely. And Miko was never one to ask for help. He was always the one lending a hand. When it came to accepting help for himself, forget about it."

"Why?"

"I don't know. I could guess it probably had something to do with the way we were raised. Our dad was a bit of a prick—certainly not a contender for Father of the Year. Some of those lessons stuck with us like dog crap on our shoe. I guess Miko thought he would look weak if he admitted he was in over his head. Maybe he heard our dad's voice berating him for being pathetic."

She fought the urge to grasp Holden's hand in a show of solidarity. Instead, she folded her hands in her lap in a deliberate motion but confessed, "I know what it's like to live with an overbearing father." She was surprised the words fell from her mouth so easily. Nobody talked badly about The Major. He was highly respected, highly decorated—the kind of man that you wanted walking the line at Guantanamo Bay but not necessarily the man you wanted helping with your homework. "My dad used to say that sweat and tears were just weakness leaving the body. But while sweat was allowed, tears were not. It was a tough way to grow up."

"I'd heard stories about your father. When he was on active duty, he had the ability to make or break careers. Based on what I know of him, he doesn't seem the kind of man who read his kids bedtime stories."

She laughed derisively. "*Au contraire.* My father loved reading World War II historical documents to us. He said it was good for the mind to learn from the mistakes of the past. My father was a big fan of military strategy."

"Historical documents...sounds kind of dry. That would put me right to sleep."

"Oh, you weren't allowed to sleep. Are you kidding? If The Major saw you nodding off, you had to do twenty push-ups."

"Damn, that's rough." He cast her a sideways glance. "Let me guess, you fell asleep fairly often...."

She frowned. "Why? Because I'm a girl? Why would you say that?"

He chuckled at her defensiveness. "Calm down, she-cat. I was just saying you're in pretty good shape and have been since I've known you, so you must've been accustomed to doing push-ups fairly regularly."

She blushed. Why did she have to jump to the wrong conclusion? Had he just given her a compliment? Yep. And she'd overreacted. "Sorry. I'm a little sensitive about certain things. It's hard growing up the only girl surrounded by military men."

"What happened to your mom?"

"She left when I was 11. I guess she got tired of being a military wife."

"That's rough. Do you see her at all?"

She barked a disgusted laugh. "I don't tend to chase after people who leave me behind. It was her loss and her choice."

"True, but I could hazard a guess that your dad's

not an easy man to live with. You never had the chance to ask her why she left?"

Jane pinned him with a hard look. "I don't care why. She's a quitter, and I don't have time to figure out why she bailed. And frankly, I don't need her in my life. I'm a grown woman and past the point of needing a mother to guide me through life."

Holden dropped it, clearly sensing they were skirting a sensitive issue. Jane took a deep breath, hating she couldn't talk about her mother without getting snippy. Once, she'd seen a therapist to see if she could work out her issues. The first visit had ended badly when the therapist had suggested Jane reconnect with her mother as part of the healing process. Like that was going to happen. "Listen, I didn't mean to snap at you. I just get hot under the collar when people keep suggesting I talk to my mother. She's the one who left, not me. As far as I'm concerned, she made her bed, and she can lie in it all by her lonesome."

"So you don't know if she remarried?"

"Actually, I do know that she remarried. Not that I care. It's her life. She's welcome to it. How did we get stuck on the subject of my mother? I thought we were talking about Miko."

Holden spread his fingers in a conciliatory manner. "Just trying to get to know my partner. And so far I know that she does not like talking about her mother."

Jane smiled. "Very astute. Your investigative skills are top-notch. Now, back to Miko. You say that justice was an important theme in his life. Maybe Miko was working undercover, trying to get enough evidence to take down I.D."

"That would make more sense than my brother just shooting himself because of a guilty conscience. I can also see him taking his own life if he thought it would protect mine. Maybe someone threatened my life and Miko did what he had to do to protect me."

"But why would someone threaten your life? You haven't had anything to do with Tessara Pharm, right?"

"No, but someone might've known Miko well enough to know that he'd do anything for me. Pulling strings with that kind of leverage would've been easy."

Jane let the information sink in for a minute. In her mind, she saw two brothers, linked by blood and soul. She wished she had that kind of connection with another human being. Growing up, her brothers had been protective, but they'd been too consumed with following in The Major's footsteps, both in career and mindset, to truly let her into their circle. Somehow, as a woman, she'd always been made to feel second best when it came to the men in her family. Had her mother felt that way, too? "You're lucky to have someone who loved you that much," she murmured, the sentiment slipping out before she could stop it. She caught Holden's questioning gaze and she shook her head. *Leave it.* "Forget I said that. I'm just tired."

To his credit, Holden didn't pry, although she saw the questions behind his eyes, and when she decided she'd try for that nap after all, he let her. Her last thought before falling into a fitful sleep was that if she wasn't careful, she'd end up seeing Holden as more than just another uniform…and that wouldn't do at all.

Chapter 9

Holden and Jane arrived at Nathan and Jaci's place around 10:00 p.m., and though Holden was sore from sitting in a plane for eight hours and it was really 1:00 a.m. in D.C., he was happy to see Nathan again after so much time. Technically, Nathan had been Miko's buddy, but Holden also considered Nathan his friend. He caught Nathan in a manly hug and clapped him on the back in a solid greeting, "Hey, ugly! The last time I saw you, you were leading us into certain death. Good times. Everything good?"

Nathan grinned. "After surviving multiple attempts on my life, rescuing my brother from a government compound and pretty much kissing away any semblance of a normal life…yeah, life is pretty good." As his gaze flicked to Jane, he said, "And you must be the investigating agent, Jane Fallon. I'd like to say it's a pleasure, but the circumstances suck."

"No offense taken," Jane said. "I wish we were meeting socially rather than officially. You seem like a decent guy."

"Don't let my rugged good looks fool you—I'm as bad as they come," Nathan said with a completely straight face, but Holden wasn't so restrained, and guffawed. Nathan turned to punch Holden in the arm. "Hey! Stop ruining my street cred. I've got a reputation to uphold."

"I didn't know you had a flair for fiction," Holden said. "Maybe you missed your calling." He gestured to the house. "Are we going to freeze our asses off outside or go inside for a beer?"

"Depends. Are you housebroken?" Nathan asked. "The last time I invited you over for a beer, you pissed in my plant."

Holden looked to Jane, who wore a faintly bemused expression. "Nathan loves to tell that story, but he fails to share that we were both drunk off our asses that night, and how was I supposed to tell a giant potted plant from the latrine? It was years ago in another country, I might add."

"You peed in a plant?"

"He killed it, too," Nathan supplied with mock seriousness. "You know, Holden, you might consider drinking more water. Your piss was so concentrated it came out as a solid."

"Shut up," Holden said, and pushed the joker as he laughed.

"All right, come on in. Jaci thought you guys would be hungry, so she kept the spaghetti warm."

"Home-cooked meal," Holden said, grinning from ear to ear. "Now, that's some hospitality."

"You'd better wait until you taste the spaghetti before you start throwing out thank-yous," Nathan warned in a conspiratorial whisper. "Jaci is on this gluten-free kick. The noodles are a bit chewy."

"Can't be any worse than an MRE," Jane said, smiling.

"You would think, huh?" Nathan countered as they walked inside, but the moment they entered the living room, his smiled widened with pure love at the sight of Jaci. Holden felt a pang of envy for what his friend had. Jaci had changed Nathan—in a good way—and it was something to see in action. Holden loved the ladies, but the idea of being tied down permanently caused sweat to break out on his forehead.

His gaze swung to Jane, and his heartbeat kicked up a notch for no good reason. Sure, she was hot— he'd have to be blind to miss her perfectly sculpted body honed by hours of gym time—but Jane wasn't a good time…in any sense of the word. Before he and Jane had hooked up, he'd always preferred his women pliable and a little dumb. That had all changed after Jane. She made him realize that smart women were more exciting, more challenging and definitely sexier than the vapid types he'd been sharing time with. He'd quickly discovered that Jane was probably smarter than he was, and she'd kept him on his toes with her sharp mind. Even though there was no downtime with her and it was exhausting, Jane was freaking hot as hell and nothing would ever change that fact.

"Holden, it's so good to see you," Jaci said as he folded her into a hug. She was the prettiest redhead he'd ever seen. Nathan certainly had good taste. She pulled away and extended her hand to Jane with a welcoming smile. "And you must be Jane. I'm Jaci. Very nice to meet you."

"Likewise. You have a lovely home," Jane supplied with polite interest. "Thank you for agreeing to let us stay while we're in town. Your hospitality is much appreciated."

"I'd like to say she's not always this stiff, but I'd be lying. Jane lives and breathes by the regs," Holden teased, and enjoyed the flush of heat in Jane's cheeks. He liked ruffling her feathers, which was probably a bad idea, but it was strangely addicting to watch her loosen up. It made him remember what she was like in bed. He suffered a mental groan as he pushed the image out of his head. "I heard there's spaghetti?" He sniffed the air and rubbed his stomach. "Even in first class, the food isn't much to write home about."

"Oh! I'm so glad you're hungry," Jaci said, leading them to the kitchen. "You'll have to tell me what you think of this new recipe I'm trying. Did you know gluten is like poison to our systems? I'm learning all about what gluten does to the body, and it's fascinating."

"As long as it tastes good, I don't care what it's made from." He flashed a grin at Jane.

Everyone took a seat at the oak table while Jaci

bustled around getting plates ready. Within minutes, they were digging in. At first bite, Holden didn't notice anything different and tucked into a few more healthy bites, but after a few mouthfuls, he started to notice the texture and chewed more slowly. "Definitely filling," he said around a hot bite, giving a thumbs-up to Jaci, who beamed before slapping Nathan lightly on the shoulder.

"See? I told you, it's only you who notices the difference. If you'd stop being so picky, you'd forget all about the fact the noodles are made from squash."

Squash? Holden choked down the last bite. He hated squash. But like Jane said, if he could choke down an MRE, he could eat anything. Holden cleaned his plate and Jane did a serviceable job choking down her portion, too, but he could tell she wasn't loving it. Jane would never be so rude as to admit she didn't like it, and Holden had to give her props for being a good sport. He'd have to take her out for some fancy coffee drink tomorrow morning, his treat. All too soon, the conversation turned serious, but he supposed there was no getting around that because it was the whole reason they'd come to California.

"So tell me what's really going on," Nathan said, playing with the wrapper on his beer. "I know you're not here for social reasons."

"I told you I thought Miko was being pushed by someone else. Someone compelled him to end his life, and I aim to find out who."

Nathan lost his easy smile. Talking about Miko was hard for them all, but more so for Nathan because he had been there when Miko ate a bullet. "Look, more than anyone I want to believe Miko wasn't the sniper who took out Tom and all those innocent people, but I just don't see who else could be pulling the strings to make that happen. Penny is dead. She was the head of the monster—I.D.—and it's over."

"It's not over," Holden disagreed with an adamant shake of his head. "Think about it, Nathan. Was Miko the kind of man who killed innocent people? He was Captain America, for crying out loud."

"We didn't know they were innocent," Nathan said, trying to get Holden to understand. "We thought we were doing a service to our country. We had no idea that Penny was the one calling the shots and running I.D. as her own personal hit squad. It's not Miko's fault. We were both duped."

"What if Miko was working undercover to expose the true head of the beast?" Holden supplied, leaning forward. "Tell me if this sounds odd…. Ulysses Rocha, an executive at Tessara Pharm, came to my boss to inquire about the status of Miko's case mere days after Chief Harris had given us a soft okay to reopen it on a temporary basis. How the hell did Rocha even know the case had been reopened?"

"I don't know," Nathan admitted, looking troubled. "Did he say anything else?"

"Just that he was there to protect the shareholders' interests and suggested the case remain shut for the greater good."

"Only someone with something to hide would balk

at the case reopening, particularly if they thought they were in the clear."

Jaci, who'd unfortunately also been present at the time of Miko's death, spoke up. "Holden, even if you're right, what good will come of this? What if the beast you're so keen on exposing is bigger than you can possibly handle? Maybe Miko realized this and that's why he took his life."

"Maybe, but that's not who Miko was. He never backed down from a fight. Even when he should've."

"You didn't see him that day," Jaci said gently. "He couldn't hide the pain in his eyes. He was eaten with guilt. Whatever his role was, he'd reached the end of his rope and checked out."

"We found three passports, cash and IDs in a hidden location in his bar," Jane jumped in, surprising Holden. The firm set of her mouth and tilt of her chin suggested she believed Holden was right. Something shifted inside of him, aligning in a new position. He thanked her silently and Jane gave an imperceptible nod before continuing in a strong, clear voice, "We think there may be a bigger connection to Tessara than previously believed. Why else would a bigwig fly all the way to Washington for a sit-down with our chief if not to send home the message that people are watching?"

"That's a good point," Nathan allowed, a dark scowl forming on his brow. "Damn that place. They ought to burn it to the ground."

Knowing Nathan's animosity toward Tessara was

centered on his brother Jake's situation, Holden asked, "Jake getting better?"

"Yeah, he's about eighty percent right now. Kat seems to think he'll make a full recovery eventually, but it's hard watching him struggle with his memory. Personally, I question the decision to keep MCX-209 in cold storage when it should've been destroyed. That drug is a threat to everyone on this planet."

Holden agreed. At Jane's questioning look, Holden explained quickly, "Jake was given a dose of an experimental drug created in a Tessara lab called MCX-209. It was supposed to cure Alzheimer's, but instead it wipes out memories. In earlier trials of the drug, it pretty much reduced the test subject to a drooling mess, or worse, dead with their brains leaking from their ears." Jane grimaced and Holden continued. "Yeah, pretty nasty stuff. The worst part is Jake's girlfriend, Dr. Kat Odgers, actually created the drug and was the one forced by a rogue faction within a government branch to administer it to him. So, understandably, no one at this table has fond feelings toward Tessara."

The color drained from Jane's face. "Why wasn't it destroyed? A drug like that…it's too dangerous for anyone to have."

"Because it's quite possibly the most innovative weapon ever created to date, and of course, our government felt it necessary to control it."

"That doesn't fill me with confidence." She shuddered a little. "Sounds like something out of a movie—and not a feel-good movie."

"Agreed," Holden said. "Back to Miko... Listen, Nathan, Jaci, it's late and we're tired. Tomorrow we're going to drop by Tessara and poke around, but in the meantime, I want you guys to search your memories and see if there's anything else you can remember about that day. Miko was stashing money and IDs for a reason. We just have to find out what it was."

They nodded, although both didn't look happy about the idea of revisiting Miko's death, not that Holden blamed them. If he'd seen his brother kill himself, he might still be in a padded cell. "Thanks. I appreciate your help."

"Anything for Miko," Nathan said. "I don't care what they say—he was a good man."

Holden blinked back tears for his friend's solidarity. No more words were needed.

Time to put a pin in this night. Tomorrow would be here in a blink.

Chapter 10

They arrived at Tessara around noon and walked into the smart building with its gleaming glass and stately metal accents.

"Someone didn't spare any expense in the decor department," Jane said, whistling beneath her breath. "Pharmaceuticals must be big business."

"Yeah, apparently big enough to fund your own personal hit squad," Holden said, clearly referencing Penny Winslow. "Honestly, I don't understand why Tessara Pharm still has government contracts. I would think this place would be like poison in the eyes of the U.S. government, seeing as one of their top executives was as corrupt as they come."

"Well, when you have the world's best and brightest working for you, those little blemishes can be overlooked, apparently," Jane responded with dry amusement.

Holden grunted in agreement. "Get ready to be politely stonewalled," he said as an impeccably dressed woman in a pencil skirt and pristine white blouse walked toward them with a pleasant smile. Both he and Jane flashed their badges, and the woman extended a cool hand first to Holden and then Jane.

"Hello. My name is Selena Weston. Welcome to Tessara Pharmaceuticals."

"Thank you for agreeing to meet with us. My name is agent Holden Archangelo and this is my partner, Jane Fallon."

"We're always happy to help as we enjoy a good working relationship with many government agencies," Selena said, revealing a row of perfectly white teeth that looked almost fake and made Jane feel self-conscious about her own teeth. Hell, everything about the woman made Jane want to freshen up, even though she knew the feeling was ridiculous. Maybe if the woman didn't have the flawless skin of a baby or the impossible figure of a Barbie doll. "If you would just follow me..."

The woman spun on her heel, drawing Holden and Jane away from the main lobby and into a private conference room with plush carpeting and a large cherrywood table surrounded by Italian leather chairs. "Please help yourself to a beverage and snacks. Mr. Rocha will be with you momentarily."

The woman exited the conference room, closing the door softly behind her. When Holden's gaze didn't linger in the woman's direction, Jane suppressed a happy smile. "Not your type?" she asked casually, as if making conversation to kill time.

"What? Plastic girl? No. Not enough muscle, and definitely not enough substance. I like a girl who can best me in the gym or collapse trying."

That smile she'd been suppressing peeped through. Jane was ridiculously charmed by the fact he was plainly referencing her. "Good to know."

"Yeah? You gonna fix me up with someone?"

Her smile disappeared. "No," she answered with a tiny bit of a growl, and he chuckled at her knee-jerk reaction. Two can play that game. "I wouldn't want to subject any of my friends to you because I'd like to remain friends with them. Any matchmaking you'll have to manage on your own."

"Little kitty has her claws out," he said with a low, amused whistle. "I'd love to pursue this conversation later, perhaps over a glass of wine?"

"In your dreams, Archangelo." Time to switch the subject. "So we're meeting with Rocha? This should be interesting."

"What'll be more interesting is what Rocha will share."

"We both know nothing is the likely answer. And right now he's listening to our entire conversation, I'll wager."

"Of course. Why else bring us to a specific room and make us wait? Typical and a little cliché. Someone has been watching too many movies."

She smiled just as a door with an invisible seam

opened in the wall and Rocha stepped out, giving Jane a momentary fright. She frowned to cover her surprise and straightened her jacket. "Tessara Pharma's full of surprises, I see," she said in a cool tone. "I didn't realize secret doors and passageways were part of standard architecture for a pharmaceutical company."

Rocha smiled. "It's a unique building. Came with the standard government-issue listening devices, too."

Aah, he had *been listening.*

"Trying to get ahead of the pharmaceutical espionage? I didn't realize finding the next best allergy medication is so cutthroat," she said. Rocha only deepened his patronizing smile. Jane wanted to punch that smug look off his face, but Reed's stern admonition rang in her ears: *Keep things civil and don't ruffle feathers.* So she supposed it was time to play civil. "Thank you for meeting us. I can appreciate your busy schedule." She shot Holden a wry look.

Rocha took a seat in the big comfy leather chair at the head of the table and gestured, encouraging them to do the same. " To what do I owe this pleasant surprise? It isn't often we get agents asking questions around here. Most of the time all we see are more members of the geek squad. Very smart, but between them couldn't lift a fully loaded sandwich."

Holden and Jane both offered a small smile in deference to his attempt at humor, but Jane could tell from Holden's determined expression he was ready to jump in feetfirst, and that suited her just fine. "We know you came to Washington to discuss the Miko

Archangelo case. First, we'd like to know how you came by such classified information. Second, we would like to know why Tessara Pharm would possibly care about that particular investigation."

Rocha leaned back in his chair. "As you know, we handle and facilitate many government contracts. I feel safe in saying that we are the premier pharmaceutical lab, handling ninety percent of the government's clandestine chemical needs. The situation involving Penny Winslow and Miko Archangelo was a black eye to Tessara. Our stocks took a hit and our investors got nervous. We've worked hard to mitigate that unfortunate circumstance so, of course, we were less than thrilled when we heard the investigation had not been closed entirely. And frankly, it's our belief that it was an error in judgment to allow a distraught family member to reopen the case when it'd been satisfactorily investigated and closed."

"That doesn't answer the question of how you came across the information," Holden maintained stubbornly, ignoring the dig. "This is a classified investigation. You should not have access to any of that information."

But Rocha wasn't in the mood to satisfy their curiosity. Instead, he said, "Would you like a tour of the facility? We are proud of the work done here. Innovative, groundbreaking, brilliant work happens on these premises. Work far more involved than manufacturing the latest and greatest allergy medication." He smiled at Jane. "I would consider it a true pleasure to escort you around the grounds. The north side is quite scenic with the manmade lake."

"That won't be necessary. We're not here as tourists," Jane said, irritated at being treated like children who were easily distracted. "We'd like to see Penny Winslow's personnel file."

Rocha shook his head with a look of chagrin. "Not without a warrant. I hate to be a stickler for the rules, but even in death we strive to protect the privacy of our people."

Holden leaned across the table. "You know I don't need a warrant to see her personnel file because she's dead. I would consider your cooperation a point in your favor that Tessara has nothing to hide, and I'm sure that will be taken into consideration when it comes time to award new contracts." Holden drummed his finger on the table. "I can appreciate how embarrassed Tessara must've been with the whole Penny Winslow situation, but we may be dealing with a bigger threat, and your cooperation would be greatly appreciated."

"I see." Rocha steepled his fingers. "And if I let you see Penny's file, what do you think you'll find?"

"I'm not sure," Jane cut in. "But I think it's safe to say that Penny was a far more complex woman than any of you imagined. We'd also like to see all projects that she personally oversaw."

"I'm not sure Penny was actively involved in any projects," Rocha said. "The executive branch rarely had personal dealings with ongoing projects."

"Even so, something tells me Penny was very

hands-on. From what I know of her, she liked to stick her fingers in all sorts of pies," Holden said.

Rocha looked cornered but conceded with grace. "I'll have the files collected. Was there anything else I can help you with?"

Holden's eyes glittered. "Just one more thing—keep your nose out of our investigation," Holden instructed with false cheer. He looked more dangerous wearing a smile than holding a gun. "The next time you come poking around where you don't belong, you might find yourself out in the cold. Catch my drift?"

Rocha chuckled as if Holden's threat was faintly amusing, but he nodded. "Sure. And now if I may, a little advice from one former military man to another—careful where you step. You never know where the next mine might be." Rocha rose and bowed slightly. "Now, if you'll excuse me, I have work to attend. Selena will see to all of your needs."

The invisible door opened with a soft *snick* and Rocha disappeared behind it. Jane and Holden shared a look before she admitted, "I totally want to see where that door goes." Then she added with a wry twist of her mouth, "And damn him for having a cool secret door. I thought only castles had those."

Holden didn't share her amusement. He dropped the cold congeniality and a darkness filled his gaze. "That man knows more than he's telling."

Jane stopped joking around to agree. "Yes, but unless we find something to work with, he's not going to voluntarily spill what he knows."

Selena appeared, impossibly pretty and perfect,

and Jane almost quipped that the woman was probably made in a lab on the fourth floor. She kept her lip zipped, though, when Selena supplied the files they'd requested. "Mr. Rocha said you may take these copies with you. Is there anything else you require?" she asked politely, clasping her hands in front of her and waiting.

"We'll be in touch," Holden said, scooping up the files.

"We look forward to your next visit. Perhaps next time you can enjoy a walk around the lake. It's so pretty."

Selena led them out of the building and waited until they were in the car to disappear back inside Tessara Pharma. Jane turned to Holden. "That was weird, right?"

"Very."

"Tessara…they don't, like, create people, right? That's not even possible. Please tell me that's not possible."

"Who knows what they do in that building. All I know is that place houses something bad and it's up to us to figure out how it's all connected."

Jane nodded, but a pinch of tension followed. "People connected to Tessara end up dead. Let's not become part of the body count."

Holden put the car in Drive, and it wasn't until Tessara was in their rearview window that Jane could breathe again.

Chapter 11

When they returned to Nathan's house, they were in a lengthy discussion about the creepy factor of Selena the robo-babe when Nathan and Jaci walked into the living room to greet them. The worried tension in Jaci's expression immediately made Holden wary. Something was going down. "Everything okay?" he asked. "You look like you're about to be the bearer of bad news."

"Can we talk to you for a minute?" Jaci asked.

Nathan wore a different kind of tension, and when he reached for Jaci's hand in a show of support, Holden was momentarily envious of their devotion to one another. It must be amazing to have someone always watching your back, no matter what. Almost without thought, his gaze strayed to Jane and she seemed wary, watching the exchange with open speculation.

"Let's do this over a beer," Nathan said, going to the kitchen to grab a few cold ones. "There's no way to pretty up what has to be said, but it'll sure as hell go down a lot easier with a little alcohol."

"Sounds serious. Are you dying?" Holden quipped, a tingle of apprehension jangling his nerves. It wasn't like Nathan to beat around the bush, so he fully expected to find out quickly what all the fuss was about.

"Not dying. At least not yet, and I'd like to keep it that way."

"You and me both, brother." Holden swigged his beer, taking a moment to enjoy the crisp taste. "So out with it. What's up your tail?"

"It's not him. It's me," Jaci said, coming clean as she folded her arms across her chest. "I don't want to sound like a jerk, but I'm scared about this investigation into Miko's case and where it might lead. I don't want Nathan to get caught up in your search for the truth."

"I tried to tell her nothing's going to happen to me," Nathan said. "But she has the right to be concerned. Some hinky stuff has happened when Tessara is involved."

"Your concerns may be warranted," Jane said gravely. "I understand your anxiety. However, there's an equal chance we won't dig up anything and this investigation will end as it started—with Miko declared guilty of treason."

"Yeah, we get it," Holden grumbled, hating the

possibility. He understood where Jaci was coming from. She and Nathan had gone through hell the last time Tessara was involved, and if Tessara was truly involved again, who knew what lengths they'd go to protect their secrets?

Nathan spoke up, looking intensely uncomfortable. "Listen, I'm not asking you to give up, but Jaci has a good point. What if there's a bigger threat? Both my brother and I almost died the last time we went up against Tessara. Jaci doesn't want me to take that chance again."

"I get it, man. I do," Holden assured Nathan, because the guy looked like he was ready to vomit. It wasn't because Nathan was scared but because he thought he was taking the coward's way out and Holden knew it. The code of honor was ingrained in them all. "There's no judgment. This could be dangerous. I shouldn't have involved you. It's my fault."

"It's just that, look what happened to Jake," Jaci said, miserable. "He's never going to be the same. People who tangle with Tessara come out dead or damaged. And I don't want that to happen to either of us or *you*. Have you even thought of that? You might have a huge target on your back just for poking around."

Holden couldn't argue with Jaci's logic. It was true Tessara had a long reach.

Jane jumped in before he could. "We don't even know that Tessara is actually involved," she said gently, trying to calm Jaci's fears. "Penny Winslow is the only connection to Tessara at this point. We could be wrong and there is no big conspiracy…just a sad story of a man with a guilty conscience."

But Jaci shook her head. "As much as I want to believe that, my gut says something else. I have a bad feeling about this investigation. Let's just say, for argument's sake, that Holden is right. There's a possibility that the person actually pulling the strings is far more dangerous than Penny Winslow ever was. And if Nathan almost died going up against her—who was a lesser threat—what does that say for this newer threat? It scares me, Holden. Not just for me and Nathan, but for you, too."

"Miko was my closest friend," Nathan said. "He always had my back and he protected me when everything turned to shit. I know I owe him more than what I'm doing and that makes me want to punch myself in the face." Nathan folded Jaci into his arms, holding her tight before continuing. "But I have to think of Jaci's safety, too. We're planning on starting a family soon, and the threat hovering over our heads with you here…it's more than I can allow. I'm sorry, man."

"No apologies needed," Holden told Nathan, shaking his head, feeling for his friend's predicament. "I know you always had Miko's back and he wouldn't want you to put your life in danger over something he'd done."

Jaci's eyes sparkled with tears. "I'm sorry. I don't want to be harsh because you seem like a good guy, but I didn't know Miko and I barely know you. All I know is that I love this man right here and the thought of losing him for someone else's fight is something

I can't handle. That's not fair to either of us. I want a normal life, one that isn't punctuated by moments of sheer terror because someone is trying to kill us. And now that I've said that, I sound totally selfish, don't I?"

"No, you don't," Jane said. "You have every right to assert your feelings into this situation. If I were you, I would, too. There's potentially a lot at stake. And you've already been through enough. No one would fault you for wanting to step outside the ring for this fight."

"You sure?" Jaci asked, sniffing back tears. "I wish I was more badass, like you. Then maybe I wouldn't so scared."

Nathan pulled away with mock incredulousness. "What are you talking about? When we were holed up in the cabin and our safe house had been made, you beaned a guy with a frying pan. I'd say that's pretty badass. We might be dead if not for your quick thinking."

Jaci giggled in spite of the gravity of the conversation, and once again Holden was envious of their bond. Damn, he was turning into a weepy woman. Holden finished his beer and placed the empty bottle on the counter. "That does sound pretty badass to me."

"Oh, my God, you guys know how to soothe a woman's ego," Jaci said, smiling, then added with the tiniest amount of pride, "It was pretty awesome."

Nathan hugged her tightly. "Damn straight."

The tension broken, Jaci said, "When times are

different, you're totally welcome in our house, I promise. I'll even cook dinner and make a pie, but until then…you're going to have to take your spy stuff elsewhere, okay?"

"Can you recommend a good hotel?" Jane asked.

"That I can do," Jaci said, brightening. "Come with me."

While Jane and Jaci hunted down a suitable hotel, Nathan and Holden went to the garage to pound down another beer, taking advantage of the bro time. "You know I feel like shit turning you out like this," Nathan admitted.

"Don't worry about it. It's nothing to lose sleep over."

Nathan shook his head. "I want you to find the answers you're looking for, but I'm in a lose-lose situation. On one hand, I want there to be a bigger answer, something other than what we know to account for Miko's actions. But if that's the case, then that means a bigger threat is hanging over all of us. And I have to protect Jaci."

"Want to know a secret?" Holden asked, pausing for a second. "I envy what you have with Jaci."

"Yeah? You, the lone wolf?"

"Hey, as I recall, you were a card-carrying member of the lone-wolf club, too," Holden said with a smirk.

Nathan laughed. "So what's the deal with you and Fallon?"

"Deal? No deal. We're partners."

"Nothing else?"

"Naw. She's all business, and hooking up with her is the last thing I need right now. I mean, she's hot but comes with too much baggage."

"Baggage? I sense a story. You've already hooked up, haven't you?"

He grinned, unable to deny it, but his smile faded quickly enough. "Listen, don't say anything. We didn't part on good terms and it's hard enough working together without our past mucking things up."

"Hey, I understand. You got feelings for her?"

"Whoa! Where'd that come from?" Holden asked with nervous laughter. "Feelings? Sure, she's my partner and I'd take a bullet for her. That's what you're supposed to do for your partner. Do I want to pick out China patterns together? No." He rolled his eyes at the thought. "We'd end up shooting each other in the housewares aisle." He finished the conversation with "She's difficult," and left it at that.

"The best ones always are. Did I ever tell you how Jaci and I got back together?"

"No. Is it a long story? Because I bore easily," he quipped.

"Shut up and listen. It's a good story. You'll love it. And if you don't love it, too bad—you're listening anyway. Okay, so there was a hit out on her—"

"Ah, the way all good love stories start," Holden interrupted with a grin.

Nathan snickered, saying, "I know, right? Anyway, there's a hit on her life and I basically kidnap her moments before the hitter buries a bullet in her skull, just like he'd done her best friend seconds earlier."

"Jeez, Nathan, this is one helluva story. You might want to edit out the gore when you tell your future kids about how Mommy and Daddy met."

"Yeah, yeah, good advice. My point? She freaking hated me because I did some messed-up shit in a backward attempt at protecting her and, well, ultimately she was unable to resist my manly charms and the rest is history. The thing is, chemistry won't be denied, no matter what you try to do to squelch it and you, my friend, and your partner...you've got chemistry. I can see it coming off you in waves. Like pheromones and shit. That stuff's real, you know."

"Thank you, Love Doctor. I had no idea you were so versed in human biology. Chemistry or not, she's got issues that I don't think I can handle."

"Such as?"

"For starters? Her dad."

"Who's her dad?"

"Brace yourself—retired Major General Gregory Fallon."

Nathan whistled in recognition, then shook his head in commiseration. "Damn, that sucks. I heard that man keeps a box of other men's testicles as war prizes. Highly decorated and scary as hell...that's a tough break. I take it a meet with the pops didn't go so well?"

"You could say that. Anyway, there's no future between me and Fallon. I don't have time for that kind of drama."

"Yeah, I hear you. However," Nathan added with a shrug, "if I'd given up on Jaci the first time she punched me in the face, I would never have the love of my life right now."

Holden rolled his eyes, a moment of disquiet filling him. Should he have fought harder for Jane when they'd broken up? Maybe he'd run too quickly. Hell, maybe if he'd stood his ground, they might've found a way around that mountain of opposition known as The Major. Then again, maybe not. Maybe it would've ended the same way, only later and with more damage.

"Thanks for the pep talk—I think. I need to ask you something related to the case. You up to answering a few serious questions?"

"Sure, buddy. It's the least I can do after tossing you out on your ear."

"Did you happen to remember anything from that day, anything you didn't tell Jane when she interviewed you?"

Nathan's smile dimmed as he shook his head. "I've been racking my brain, trying to remember every detail. But everything I can remember I've already told Jane for her report."

"I appreciate you trying." Holden finished his beer. "We visited Tessara today. We have some reading material to go over."

"Should I even ask?" Nathan asked. "I can't believe they let you walk out with personnel files."

"Yeah, well, I can't tell if they're trying to cooperate or if they're trying to throw us off the scent. Either way, I'm interested in seeing what Penny Winslow had her fingers on."

"Knowing that sneaky bitch, she probably had her fingers on everything. She was not only greedy, but also consumed with her own ego. To this day, I'll never know what Tom saw in her."

"The heart is often blind," Holden said softly. "I'd say he paid for his error in judgment."

Nathan nodded. That was all that needed to be said about that. Tom Wyatt had been like a father figure to Nathan, and when he had been implicated in the illegal activities, it had damn near broken Nathan's heart. To make matters worse, Nathan had been in the room when a sniper took out Tom in his own den with a single bullet whizzing through the glass straight to the man's skull. A perfect hit. Tom was also on Miko's list of crimes.

Nathan settled a reassuring hand on Holden's shoulder. "Hey, try to remember that even if you're wrong and Miko is truly guilty of everything he's been accused of, he was still your brother and my friend. And we knew him as a good man. Nothing can take that from us."

Holden nodded, appreciating his friend's quiet wisdom. "Me and Jane better get to the hotel so we can start going over the Tessara files," he said, giving himself the chance to exit gracefully.

Nathan and Holden embraced like men—rough and hard—and then sprang apart with quick good-byes.

Once in the car, Jane looked to Holden. "You okay?

You two were in the garage for a while. I was starting to run out of things to talk about with Jaci. She's nice, but we don't really have a lot in common."

"Yeah I can imagine—the graphic designer and the hard-core marine. It's not as if you'd run in similar circles." Holden sighed as he rubbed his brow. "I don't blame Nathan. He did what he had to do. If I had someone I cared about and that person was threatened, I'd do the same."

"Growing up in a military family, it's hard to imagine living as a civilian. Weapons training, PT and hand-to-hand combat training has been part of my life since I was a kid. It must've been terrifying to go through what Jaci did with zero training."

"Yeah, but she held her own in the end from what Nathan told me. Same with Kat, Jake's wife. She was even more helpless. The woman had practically lived in the lab before Jake plucked her out and brought her to D.C. People grow when they have to, and I guess the strong will find a way to survive."

"Yeah, I guess so." There was something quiet and vulnerable about the way Jane said it that when she tucked a piece of hair behind her ear and turned her gaze out the window, he was struck by the knowledge that if someone were threatening Jane, he'd tear their spine out.

Nope, he didn't fault Nathan. He understood. He spotted the hotel Jaci recommended just off the highway. "We're here. Let's see if they have any vacancies."

* * *

They were able to immediately book two adjoining rooms. After ordering some Thai food for delivery, they tackled the personnel file. "Well, Holden, you are right about one thing—this woman was very hands-on. She's listed as the lead supervisor on a number of different projects." Jane pulled a highlighter from her purse and began marking the projects. "That seems a bit odd considering she was an executive, right?"

"Yes, but she was also one of the founders of Tessara. She had a biochemical engineering background."

"It says here she got her degree after serving her time in the military. I guess she was fairly brilliant," Jane said, a note of grudging respect entering her voice. "I mean, she was a total psychopath, of course. But you know what they say about geniuses—they're all a little crazy."

"That's a stereotype. I'm not crazy in the least," Holden joked, and Jane graced him with a sardonic smirk. He chuckled and balled up his napkin to toss it basketball-style in the wastebasket near the door. "She was crazy, that's for sure. So what are some of the projects?"

"Well, they all have names, which are likely code for whatever they were. So who's to say which is which or if they are connected to Miko?"

"At this point I think we have to grasp at any straw thrown our way."

Jane nodded. "Okay, so some of the project names

are Switchblade, Carousel, Serenade, Game Changer." She looked up. "Any of those sounds familiar?"

Holden mulled over the information and then, pulling something from memory, said, "Game Changer... that's what MCX-209 was nicknamed by that freak responsible for what happened to Jake. That's how they were presenting it on the black market."

"Are you saying that Jake's girlfriend was working for Penny Winslow?"

"Not directly, I'm sure. Kat would've answered to her immediate supervisor, but that supervisor would've answered to someone else higher up the chain."

"Damn...the possibility that MCX-209 is involved gives me hives. It's like finding out that time travel is possible and a Terminator is coming to kill me. Freaky stuff."

"Kat had been working on MCX-209 for a year before all hell broke loose. I wonder if Penny was keeping close tabs on her progress."

"If she had her fingers in this pie, chances are the answer is yes. I mean, think about it, a drug that can erase memory? She would've been unstoppable." Jane shivered.

"True. It would've been a considerable asset in her arsenal. But I don't know if MCX-209 had shown any progress at that point. It would've been in its infancy of testing."

Jane tapped the marker on the file. "But if Penny had a background in biochemical engineering, she would've been able to study Kat's notes, right?"

"Yeah?" He raised an eyebrow.

"Well, maybe she knew the drug was going to fail in its original inception but found a bigger, more nefarious purpose and thus kept Kat working on it under the guise of supporting her research."

"Sounds like something that woman would do. When we get back to Washington, we should hit up Kat and see what she remembers about that time at Tessara."

"Isn't she working for the Department of Defense now?"

He nodded. "Best way to control a threat is to control its funding."

"True. I'm surprised she agreed to work for the government after everything she'd been through."

"Yeah, me, too. But she's a scientist at her core and she was given an offer she couldn't pass up. I'm not going to judge her for doing what she felt was right for herself and Jake."

"No, of course not," she said, shuffling through the paperwork and stifling a yawn. "It's been a long day. Want to call it?"

Holden didn't appear happy with that idea, but his eyes were bloodshot, too. "Yeah, I guess so." He gathered the papers he'd been studying and tidied them into a pile. "We're a good team. Who knew, right?"

She caught his gaze and her cheeks heated for no good reason. One compliment from Holden and she goes all girlie on him? *Get a grip.* Jane smiled and nodded. "Seems that when we're not fighting one another, things get done."

"Yeah." He leaned back in his chair and popped his back. "I'm feeling not being able to work out for the past few days," he said, wincing as he stretched. "Working out keeps the kinks from permanently kinking."

She tried to keep her gaze on her paperwork, as her brain was currently objectifying his body like a rabid teen at a boy-band concert. All she had to do was think of how inappropriate it was to obsess on the rugged hills and valleys of every muscular portion of his body and she could smother this raging attraction, which seemed to be getting out of control with each passing second. Yep. Any second now she'd get things under control.

Any. Second.

Her gaze found his and what she saw there mirrored the hunger she felt curling in her belly. She breathed a distressed "Oh, no…" before he suddenly pulled her to him and planted a searing kiss on her upturned, nearly puckering lips.

And that was exactly how fires raged out of control—when you threw gasoline on them.

Chapter 12

Jane melted beneath Holden's touch, all resistance and good sense following in sequential order, leaving behind nothing but raging attraction and insane, career-killing lust. Every thwarted sexual impulse and smothered tingle of desire raged in her nerve endings, demanding more and then some. If she could think straight, she would remind Holden that morning afters were awkward, and even more so when the person you'd shagged was staring at you from across the debriefing room. But who could counter with reason when there was a tongue in your mouth, twisting your resolve into a tiny, minuscule pretzel?

"You have no idea how long I've wanted to do that. I've missed you, Jane," Holden said in a husky murmur against her lips. He grabbed her hand and pulled her from the chair, spinning her around so her backside was pressed firmly against his groin. "Feel that?" His hardened erection ground against her behind, stealing her breath. "That's what you do to me no matter how much I try to forget." His hand reached around to cup her through her jeans, and she squirmed as heat flooded her body at his possessive touch.

"This is probably a bad idea," she felt obligated to say, even as she bit her lip and held back a cry when he moved the heel of his hand against her. "This doesn't change anything if we do this. Coworkers only, right?"

"Of course," he said, nibbling her neck and sucking the flesh between his lips for a sharp bite. They walked slowly backward, and Holden gave her a hard push onto the bed. She gasped as he towered over her with that damnably sexy grin. She reached up and jerked him to her, obliterating that grin beneath the onslaught of her mouth. Their tongues tangled, fighting for dominance, leaving them both breathless and desperate to shuck their clothes. They wasted no time. Within seconds, the sound of ripping fabric and popping buttons filled the air. In a heartbeat, their naked bodies were sliding against one another in a gloriously dirty dance that left them both growling as they pushed one another to deeper, more complete absolution. Holden took care of the protection, impatiently sliding a condom onto his shaft before filling and stretching her with delicious intent. *Good God,* she thought dizzily, clinging to him. She'd missed this! She gasped as the head of his shaft punched that sweet spot with unerring accuracy, sending her into shuddering orbit as he did it again and again, demanding that she take every inch until she was no longer aware where he stopped and she began. An animalistic groan popped from her mouth when he stopped to flip her around to her belly. She arched her back with a hiss as he slid back inside her slick heat. She couldn't help herself, rocking and writhing against his shaft, taking her pleasure as surely as he was taking his own.

"Holden," she gasped his name like a prayer, begging for release, but he wasn't ready to give it to her. He was drawing it out, milking the moment for all it was worth, and she was thankful. They both knew this was a one-time deal, right? Might as well leave a mark to make it count. "Oh…Holden, please…"

"Not yet, sweet Janey," he said, squeezing her cheeks as he drove into her flesh, making her shake with each thrust. She groaned, then cried out in frustration when he withdrew again to roll her onto her backside. "What are you d—"

And then she sucked in a wild cry as his mouth descended between her folds, teasing that secret pleasure button, demanding her surrender without mercy. She couldn't run, couldn't hide from the pleasure that was building. And she didn't want to. She wanted it all. She wanted the pain, the sweetness, the delectable forbidden nature of everything they were doing together. At that moment, she wasn't the good girl, the perfect daughter who always made the decisions that would reflect well on her family. She was a wanton, sex-starved she-devil who wanted destruction and mayhem as much as she craved acceptance and praise. Dual natures clashed and she thrashed, gripping the bedsheet between her sweaty palms. When he lightly grazed his teeth across her hood and slipped his finger deep inside her, she shattered with a keening cry that surely the entire hotel heard, every muscle clenching in glorious unison, toes curling hard enough to start a cramp. Her breath left her lungs until they threatened to collapse. "H-Holden," she gasped, her head lolling to the side as her eyes glazed in postorgasmic bliss. "Holden…" It was all she could manage. But the blaze of hunger in his eyes told her this ride was just beginning. Before she could fully recover, Holden was inside her again; this time, he was going to push her harder than ever. It would be a miracle if she could walk by morning.

Sweat slicked their bodies as Holden worked himself back into Jane's hot core, gritting his teeth at the insane, delicious pressure ricocheting down his shaft and pooling in his balls. This was crazy, his brain bubbled with maniacal glee, but he was desperate to touch every inch of her honeyed skin. Maybe it was experiencing the tender bond between Nathan and Jaci that had ignited this fierce hunger inside him. Whatever the reason, he couldn't stop himself. Jane was toned, with feminine curves for a man to hold on to. Her hips flared in the most achingly perfect way, and he wanted to lose himself between her folds to devour her taste. It was a bad idea—all of this—but did that matter? Hell no! When he saw that dark look in her eyes, that split second of raw yearning peeking through the curtain of self-possessed reserve that she always maintained, he had lost it and stolen the moment. Maybe he'd live to regret it. Who cared? He was with her now and it was everything he remembered it to be.

He'd brought her to release once, but that wasn't enough. He wanted to make sure that when she closed her eyes at night, she thought of him and all the things he'd done to her. Maybe it was egotistical—okay, yeah, it was—but for some reason, he wanted to be the only man she remembered in her private thoughts. He wanted to dominate her fantasies until only he remained. What did that mean? He'd never cared before with his other lovers, but Jane had been a tough habit to quit cold turkey. In the past, he'd been happy to share and share alike. But not with Jane. The very idea of Jane being with someone else caused a growl to rumble from his chest, and he renewed his efforts to leave a brand on her soul.

"Holden, oh, Holden…" she breathed, clinging to him with her legs wrapped tightly around his torso as he drove into her without mercy. Her eyes were squeezed shut and he swept her mouth with his tongue, forcing her to remain in the here and now with him. She tensed and began to shake, and he knew the moment was here.

"Open your eyes, sweetheart," he instructed, needing to know that the moment she came, she'd know exactly who'd brought her to that sweet release. Her eyes popped open and she stared into his, gasping as she tumbled for the second time into a hard orgasm. Their connection felt cosmic as they locked eyes, and within the next breath, as she was crying out, he hurtled into his own release, losing himself for several blessed moments in sheer ecstasy. Holy…hell…he'd never…not like that. He collapsed beside her, both of them breathing hard and trying to recover from whatever it was that had just taken them on an epic ride. "That was…"

"Don't talk," she panted. "Shh."

And he agreed. Words weren't necessary. Their bodies had shared something he'd never experienced with anyone else. Something mind-blowing. Something…scary. Something like *chemistry*.

Everything had changed. He couldn't agree to go back to just being partners. He'd made the mistake the first time of letting her go without a fight. His ego had been bruised and a part of him had believed what The Major had said about him not being good enough for Jane. Who was he? And what did he have to offer Jane? But in this moment, he said, screw the haters. He'd been stupid and immature to walk away just so he could lick his wounds in private. Sure, he covered pretty well with his nonchalance, but it was forced. The real reason he worked out at the same time as Jane was because it was the only time he could possibly be around her without actually admitting he still needed and wanted her. Yeah, that ego was pretty strong.

He risked a glance at Jane, her eyes closed and lips parted as her chest rose and fell from their exertion. The sheer beauty of the woman struck him like a thunderbolt splitting the sky and crashing around him.

Yeah, things had changed, all right.

And something told him there was no putting that genie back in the bottle.

Faaantastic.

Jane was going to love this.

Chapter 13

The following morning, Jane rolled to her side and started to leave the bed when Holden stirred. She winced as muscles she'd never imagined were part of her body cried out in protest. It was a delicious pain, one that reminded her of everything they'd done last night, but in the same breath, the reminder made her want to hop the first rocket to another planet. What had they done? She wanted to cover her face with her hands and die. She popped from the bed and ran to the bathroom. *What were you thinking?* She stared hard at her reflection in the mirror, noting the wild bedhead and the stubble burn on her neck from Holden's lips. A delicate shudder rocked her frame as she sank into the memory with a heavy sigh. That man could do things that weren't natural.

Snap out of it. This kind of thinking wasn't productive. She straightened and stepped away from the sink to twist the shower knob to hot. The heat would burn away the evidence and soothe her sore muscles. Win-win. Jane stepped into the shower as the steam filled the room. She closed her eyes, the water pelting her head and running in rivulets down her body. Bracing herself against the wall with her forearms, she stood for a long moment simply enjoying the feel of the water running over her.

Suddenly, hands cupped her breasts and she yelped, immediately jabbing with her elbow and connecting with a hard chest as the person behind her grunted and pulled her to him. "Stand down, soldier," he murmured, and her knees threatened to melt into gooey piles of cartilage. Holden.

"What are you doing?" she asked, trying to stay focused, but Holden was teasing her nipples between his thumb and forefinger and rational thought was becoming difficult. "I thought we agreed it was a one-time thing. We can't be shagging each other like it's no big deal."

He kissed her neck and ignored her, reaching down to plunder her folds with his finger, reminding her of everything he'd done to her last night. She whimpered and sagged against him, giving him better access even as she cursed her own weakness. "This is a terrible—*aah*—idea!"

"The worst," he agreed, slowly working his finger inside her. "And yet...I think we should keep doing it. Over and over and over."

She shuddered as a sweet orgasm caught her by surprise, cresting over her in a gentle tide, nothing like what'd happened last night, and for that, she was grateful. She needed to be able to walk. A sigh rattled out of her mouth as she leaned against Holden, who was smiling as he withdrew his finger and popped it into his mouth. "Mmm…sweet like candy," he said, causing a blush to burn her cheeks. Had he just—? Oh, such a bad boy.

He turned her around to face him as the steam swirled around their bodies. His erection bobbed between them, but he seemed more content to stand there with her, damn the consequences and screw the good sense they were both ignoring. "I don't think I can 'hit it and quit it' when it comes to you." He drew her closer so their skin touched. The heat from his body made her want to climb into his skin and live there. He was like a human furnace, which would come in handy seeing as her toes were always cold. "I know it would be smarter if I did. But there's something about you that fills me with…hell, I don't even know what the word is. All I know is now that I've tasted you again, you're the only one I want, and I should've fought harder to keep you the first time around."

Jane thrilled at the dangerous words, though she knew they had no future. For one, her brothers and father would have a fit. Holden was too tainted by his brother's crime to be a suitable match. As far as her father was concerned, only five-star generals and Purple Heart recipients need apply for the role of significant other in Jane's life. As a rule, Jane had kept her dating exploits on the down low, and with good reason. Then Holden had gone against her express wishes and tried talking to her father as if he were a normal parent, and all hell had broken loose.

"What in the world are you thinking?" she'd asked in a harsh whisper as Holden had walked with purpose to her father's doorstep. "You have lost your mind! You don't know what you're doing and this is not going to end well. Stop this, Holden!"

"This is ridiculous. I'm sure you're overreacting. He's your father, not the pope."

"Please don't say that to him," she'd muttered, rubbing her right temple. "You don't know what you're getting into. This is not the way to meet my father for the first time."

"Yeah, well, I disagree. Time to stop sneaking around. Maybe we can go shoot a couple of rounds at the range."

"Do you realize he had the last guy I dated sent to the front lines in Afghanistan because he didn't like his haircut?"

"I've been to Afghanistan—no big deal," Holden had said with a negligent shrug that she'd found half adorable and half mad. "But just to be on the safe side, how's my hair?"

"High and tight. It's fine," she'd answered, swallowing her tongue when her father had appeared at the door. She'd forced a smile and said, "Hi, Dad. We were just in the neighborhood. If you're busy…"

"We? We who?" The Major had eyed Holden with

open suspicion and borderline dislike. "Is this the man you've been seeing on the QT?"

He knows, she'd thought. Damn those military connections. She'd wondered which old fart had ratted her out. No telling; her father's reach was pretty extensive and even crossed military branches. "Um..." Her words had dried up in her mouth and unfortunately Holden had taken the opportunity to insert himself.

"Yes, sir, I'm that guy. Pleasure to meet you. I've heard of your accomplishments. Pretty impressive."

Jane had wanted to groan. Her father was incapable of succumbing to flattery, and she'd known Holden's attempts at buttering him up would only end badly. Before she had been able to interject, her father had said, "Son, where I come from it's considered very bad form to attempt to date a man's only daughter without a proper introduction. How long has this been going on?"

"A few weeks," Holden had answered, looking to Jane when he'd realized this wasn't going as smoothly as he'd planned.

"I suppose you and I are overdue a chat." The Major had opened the door wider and motioned for Holden to come in. Jane had wanted to grab Holden and tell him to run for safety, but Holden had naively followed The Major before she could stop him. Just as she'd taken the first step, her father had said, "Jane, why don't you take a jog around the block? Your last PT report was a little weak in the running department."

"Dad? I'm not exactly dressed to go for a jog," she'd protested, but she'd been more keen on extracting Holden than anything else.

But her father never accepted excuses. "I know you keep some running shoes in the car because I taught you to."

She'd nodded, caught. "Yes, sir."

"By the time you circle back around I should be finished with my chat."

"Dad…"

"That'll be all, Jane."

And then she had been dismissed as he'd closed the door, effectively locking Holden inside and her out. "Crap," she'd muttered and returned to her car. She'd grabbed her tennis shoes and jerked them on. Whatever her father had been saying to Holden hadn't been "welcome to the family, son." She'd had a bad feeling it was going to be the opposite.

And she'd been right. Jane roused herself from that terrible memory and exhaled the tight breath caught in her chest. Why hadn't Holden just listened to her for once? Maybe if he hadn't been so cocksure of himself, they might've been able to figure out a plan together, but no, he'd been absolutely certain of his ability to charm The Major, and whatever he'd said to her dad had been the catalyst that ended their relationship.

"You're suddenly really quiet," Holden observed, drawing her back to the present. "Penny for your thoughts."

"They're not worth that much," she answered, deliberately giving him her back to tease him with the view as she reached for the shampoo. After a career in the military, modesty wasn't a luxury she remembered. "I think we've gotten all we can here in California. I'd like to get back to Washington as soon as possible so we can interview Jake and Kat. Is there anything else you need here in Cali?"

"Oh, that's how it's going to be?" he asked, a hint of amusement in his voice. She half turned and didn't pretend to not know what he was talking about.

"Yes. You and I both know that what we did was a mistake. There's no need to compound matters." Her gaze dipped to his erection and she swallowed before jerking back around to scrub her hair. "Don't get me wrong, I fully enjoyed myself, but we have to get back to business and wrap up this investigation. I have other cases waiting for me."

He reached past her and grabbed the shampoo. "First, what we did may have been a mistake, but I don't regret it. Second, you're crazy if you think I'm going to be able to forget how amazing we are together between the sheets and third, I can guarantee you're going to be thinking of us before we've even left the tarmac. Just admit it—we're good together. And we always were until your control-freak daddy got in the way. When you are going to stop letting him run your life?"

"Leave my dad out of this." She spun around, irritated. "Yes, we're good together. We're both in phenomenal shape, we have similar drives and our bodies fit together extraordinarily well, but that's not the point."

"It isn't?"

"No," she answered firmly, taking the shampoo from his hands and returning it to the ledge as he scrubbed. "The point is that you and I cannot be messing around like a couple of college coeds on spring break. We cannot do anything that will jeopardize the integrity of the case—both for my sake as the lead investigator and for your sake as you search for answers. We need to just forget it happened and move on. We did it once and we can't do it again." They switched places so Holden could rinse, and she clenched her fingers to keep from touching those rock-hard ridges of abdominal muscle that gave *washboard* a new definition. "Furthermore, we already have a deficit with you being all emotional about this case, and we certainly don't need to add to the already complicated situation." His lopsided grin appeared and she glared. "Are you listening at all?"

"To the words coming out of your mouth? No, not really. But in my defense, your boobs are definitely speaking my language." And with that, he pulled her to him, smothering her protests with a bone-searing kiss that left her with jelly on the inside. She whimpered as the fight left her temporarily. "There's my sexy girl," he murmured against her lips. When he had her quiet, he stared into her half-closed eyes and said, "I don't know why it took me so long to figure out that I should've told your father to go screw himself. As soon as we touch down in D.C., that's exactly what I'm going to do."

"You'll do no such thing," she said, glaring. "That's my father you're talking about."

"Yeah, and he's been running your life for long enough, don't you think?"

"He's not running my life," she shot back, indignant. "That's a helluva thing to say to someone you're hoping to have sex with again."

"I want more than sex," he said with a straight face. "I want you."

"Stop it," she told him, irritated that his admission caused her heart rate to hop, skip and jump like an Easter bunny on meth. "You're being ridiculous and I need you to focus. Remember the case? That's our priority—not whatever drama you're cooking up in your head right now. We had a past, a history, and it didn't work out. And not because of my dad, but because we're not suited in the big scheme of things, okay?"

"I call bullshit," he said. "You pushed me out of your life because Daddy told you to."

"You're one to talk. Whatever my dad said to you that day really must've hit a nerve because you couldn't get out fast enough."

He stiffened. "He was a real jerk."

"Yeah? Well, that's who he is and who he'll always be, and if you can't handle that, you can't handle being with me for the long haul. I realized that from the start, which is why I didn't pursue what we had. Got it? It had nothing to do with my dad."

Was that a lie? Well, they say the most convincing lies are grounded in truth. She hadn't wanted to rock the boat, not when things had started to level out with her dad and she'd finally found equal footing in her career. But she'd also known that Holden would never fit in with the exclusive boys' club of her brothers and father. So why push it? A tiny, pipsqueak of a voice whispered a stark truth that she'd struggled with ever since letting Holden go—she'd had real feelings for Holden. Not the kind that came and went, but the kind that reached down into her heart and tugged hard. Pushing him away had been a painful experience. Working alongside him as if he'd been merely a pleasant diversion had been even harder. Holden called her the ice queen because she had to shut down in order to function. Maybe she ought to tell him that. Or maybe she ought to stay the course because nothing had really changed. Her father and brothers, whom she loved and respected, would never accept Holden, and that was a fact, which meant, chemistry aside, their situation remained the same. "Why can't you just enjoy this one illicit moment and then let it go?" she asked, almost plaintively.

"Because I tried that before and it only made me miserable. Let's try it my way for once," he suggested, pulling her toward him even as she shook her head at the lusty haze slowly clouding his gaze. But he plainly wouldn't take no for an answer as he said, "If I'm spending my time fighting my attraction to you, I'll have that much less energy to focus on what we're supposed to be investigating. Make sense?"

In a hazy way, yes. She nodded slowly and his grin widened. "Good. Now, let me show you the art of the shower quickie…."

"But we don't have protection," she protested weakly, her tongue already sliding along her lower lip in anticipation. But Holden had thought ahead. He reached over her to the lip of the shower wall and grabbed the condom he'd stashed there. "You devil," she said with a reluctant smile. "What if I'd kicked you out of the shower?"

"Never crossed my mind," he said, shredding the packaging and slipping on the condom. His gaze darkened as he spun her around, pulling on her hips. "Brace yourself," he instructed; seconds later, he was buried inside her.

Oh, jeez. Quickie shower sex was one helluva good workout. And she loved a good workout.

Holden slipped his shirt over his head and slid his jeans on, his mind humming with thoughts that had nothing to do with the case and everything to do with the beautiful woman he couldn't take his eyes off. "When we broke up, was it so easy to forget about me?" he asked.

"I wouldn't exactly call what we were doing dating."

"Well, difference of opinion, I suppose. Humor me and answer the question," he said, tying his shoes and standing.

"Does it matter?"

"To me it does."

She heaved a short sigh, as if irritated that he seemed fixated on the past. "No, it wasn't easy, okay? It was pretty damn hard, but when you grow up like I did, you get used to hard."

"He doesn't have to rule your life anymore," he told her, gentling his voice. "All you have to do is stand up for yourself and what you want out of life."

"Holden, stop. You don't understand the relationship I have with my family. I'm not peppering you with judgment about your dedication to your brother, so don't give me crap about how I handle my relationship with my kin, okay?"

"My old man was a drunken prick most days and yours is a control-freak drill sergeant. I'd say we share some similarities in our upbringing. The one difference? I made the choice to put my life first. Somehow you got stuck playing second fiddle to every male in your family, and I think that's messed up because any father should be proud to have a daughter like you."

She startled at the unexpected compliment, but she held to her guns. "My dad needs me. When my mom left us, we all picked up the slack. It's what you do when your family is threatened—circle the wagons. You did it with your brother, right?"

"Yeah, I did," he admitted. "It's hard for me to watch you sacrifice your happiness on someone else's authority, though. Doesn't make sense."

"I'm not unhappy."

"Yeah, keep telling yourself that, Fallon," he said with a sad shake of his head. "But if this situation with my brother has taught me anything, it's that things can change in the blink of an eye and there aren't take-backs. You get one chance in this life, so don't throw it away."

"I know."

"Doesn't seem like it. You talk a good game. Your actions tell a different story. When are you going to choose your happiness over someone else's?"

She scowled. "Are we really having this conversation? We need to get back to the case."

"We will. Answer the question."

"If you don't drop it, I'll break your fingers," she said sweetly, tucking her gun into the back of her waistband and covering it with her shirt. "Let's get back to the point of this trip, which was not to rehash the past. Got it?"

"Fair enough. Still doesn't get you off the hook. This isn't finished yet."

She barked a short laugh at his statement. "Oh, is that so? We had some good times and now those good times have come to an end. Beautiful, simple and to the point."

"Yeah, sure." He pinned her with an intense look. "Kiss before we leave our little love nest?"

"Keep dreaming, Casanova. We have a plane to catch." And then she scooped up her carry-on and sauntered out of the room. Damn, that was harsh and yet so hot.

"Move your ass, Archangelo," she called over her shoulder. "Our plane leaves in an hour." He had no choice but to follow.

He took one last lingering look around the business hotel room, with its nondescript wallpaper and neutral carpet, but all he saw was the memory of him and Jane, defiling every discernible inch in wicked fashion. "Good times," he murmured with a sad exhale to be leaving it all behind. He closed the door. Jane was right. Time to get back to work.

Chapter 14

They were buckling into the car when Holden's cell rang. "It's James," he said, and answered the call. "Hold on, buddy. You're going on speaker." He clicked his smartphone and James's voice filled the car cab.

"Sleep is overrated, and I've found that when you're in a hyperaware state, your brain actually becomes more efficient."

"That's not actually accurate," Jane murmured, shooting Holden a quick look, but he compelled her to keep quiet as James rambled to his point.

"All right. You're not going to believe what I dug up about your boy, Miko...."

"Spit it out," Holden gritted his teeth. "We've got a plane to catch."

"Well, you might want to reschedule your flight because I've got some information that might interest you."

"Why can't you just tell me now?"

"Over the phone? Over an unsecure line? What? You think I was born yesterday? I don't think so. Meet me at Café Orange on Bluebell Street in twenty minutes."

Then the line went dead. Holden rolled his eyes. "Great. It's the Geek Supremacy. This guy is too much." He looked to Jane. "Can you reschedule our flight for tonight?"

"Sure. Let's hope this guy delivers, because he sounds like a fruit loop with an overinflated sense of importance."

"Oh, he's a genius. That about sums it up."

"Yes, it does."

Holden pocketed his phone while Jane brought up the GPS. Within fifteen minutes, they were walking into the small French café and heading straight for the twitchy man nursing what was likely his third espresso.

They slid into the seats across from James, and he startled at their appearance. "Hey, I didn't realize you'd actually make it in twenty minutes."

"Fifteen with five to spare. What do you have for us?" Jane said, cutting to the chase.

"Okay, here's the deal. I did what you asked and traced the money—that was child's play—and because you're friends with Nathan and Jaci, I decided to take it a step further, nose around and see what popped up. I hacked your brother's email account and found more interesting stuff than where he has money stashed. By the way, your brother had some serious cash flow to be tucking away the amounts he's got pocketed in Mexico."

"How much?" Holden asked.

"Brace yourself…one hundred Gs. Pow! That's a lot of margaritas," James said, cocking his fingers into guns with a grin, but Holden didn't find any of this funny. James slowly dropped his finger guns and refocused after a shaky drink of his espresso. "Okay, so anyway, yeah, he's got money in all those places, but Mexico had the biggest cash drop. But that's not the interesting part. He has a safety deposit box in Washington that I think you're going to want to open."

"What's in it?"

"I don't know, but he references it as his insurance policy, and something tells me he's not talking about MetLife."

Jane and Holden shared looks, then Holden prompted, "What else did you find?"

"He kept referencing a winery outside of Washington. Mean anything to you?"

"What?" Holden was confused. "My brother didn't like wine. He was more of a Jameson guy. Why would he be talking about a winery?"

"That's your job to figure out. The winery is owned by a Trevor Granger. The name is Butterfly Bend." James took a short breath and blew it out.

"And that's all I got. When can I get the wire for the second half of my fee?"

"You'll get it when I check out your story," Holden said, looking to Jane. "Granger…that name is familiar." He snapped his fingers in quick recognition. "That's right, Penny Winslow's maiden name was Granger. Do you believe in coincidences?"

"Not really," she answered. "Guess we're going back to Tessara?"

"Bet your ass we are." He stood and looked at James. "Thanks. I'll be in touch. Oh, and, James, get some sleep. You look like shit."

They left the café and booked it back to the car, his mind moving at the speed of light. Why did it always come back to Tessara? "I feel that place is at the epicenter of all bad things," he said darkly, and Jane nodded. "Why would my brother reference a winery unless there was something behind the curtain to keep watch on?"

"I'm curious as to what's in that security box. What do you think it could be?"

"I don't know, but I'm starting to lean toward the theory that my brother was on to something and he was trying—in true Miko fashion—to take whoever it was down by himself and got in over his head."

Jane nodded slowly and added, "I definitely think there's something going on, but I don't want to jump to conclusions."

"Of course not," he said, but his heart was beating like a wild thing in his chest at the possibilities.

"Should I call Rocha and let him know we're on our way?"

"Hell no. Let's surprise him and see what happens," Holden said with a short smile. "I'd love to show up with a warrant, but we don't have enough evidence for that…yet."

"By the numbers, Holden," she warned. "Don't go all cowboy on me. If Tessara is behind shady deals, we'll figure it out the legal way. Just be patient."

Holden wasn't in the habit of issuing promises— especially ones he didn't know if he could keep. He pressed his foot harder on the gas pedal and hurtled down the freeway toward Tessara Pharmaceuticals.

When they walked into the Tessara facility, Selena immediately appeared with a faint question marring her flawless skin, though her hands were clasped in front of her with complete serenity. Jane was pretty sure she wasn't human and was tempted to check for a pulse. "We're here to speak with Mr. Rocha."

"Mr. Rocha isn't here," Selena said with an apologetic smile. "He's a very busy man. Perhaps you could make an appointment?"

"Someone else has to be running this operation," Holden said. "Bring us that person."

Selena's smile faltered and she blinked as she processed the realization that they would plant their feet and wait until someone talked to them. "I see. Come with me," she instructed, turning to take them back into the conference room with the hidden door.

"Please help yourself to snacks and beverages. Everything is organic and fresh."

"Ironic given this is a pharmaceutical company, isn't it?" Jane said to Holden as Selena left the room, gracing them with a sugary sweet smile that oddly made Jane think of a shark. "That woman ain't right," she said once they were alone.

"Agreed. I get a definite serial killer vibe from that chick. I've never been so chilled by a pretty smile."

"You think she's pretty?" Jane asked diffidently, shooting for nonchalance. "I mean, not that I care, of course. Just curious."

"Um, I sense a trap," he said, and she snorted. "Hey, I've been well schooled in the belief that there are some questions you never answer because it's a zero-sum game. As in *no winner.*"

"Oh, good grief, Holden. It was just a silly question," she said, miffed that he was right. If he'd answered yes, he thought Selena was pretty, it would've eaten at her nerves, which in turn would've pissed her off for caring in the first place. If he'd said no, then she would've believed him a liar and definitely untrustworthy. "Fine. It was a trap." She scowled, then deliberately shook off the weird vibe. "Forget I said anything. It was dumb to even ask. I don't care who you find attractive."

Holden's gaze smoldered, taking her breath away, and if they weren't on official business, she had no doubt he would've shoved her up against the nearest wall to demonstrate just how attractive he found *her.* "Oh, crap. Don't look at me like that," she warned.

He chuckled. "Mind reading is part of your skill set?" he asked.

She shot him a cool look. "You don't have to read minds to know what'd just circulated through your brain. Get it together."

The lust slowly cleared from his stare and he shrugged in his jacket, adjusting himself with admirable efficiency just in time for Ulysses Rocha to walk in. "Agents. What a pleasant surprise," he said.

"Back so soon?" Jane asked pointedly. Ulysses smiled in apology.

"Selena tries to protect my schedule. She's a good assistant. However, the minute she told me my unexpected visitors were Agents Archangelo and Fallon, I made time. What can I do for you?"

"What relation is Penelope Granger, aka Penny Winslow, to Trevor Granger?" Jane got straight to the point.

Ulysses frowned. "A cousin, I believe, if memory serves. Why?"

Neither she nor Holden answered; instead, she pushed on to their next question. "Penny Winslow was involved in a number of projects here, most notably the Game Changer, which was the nickname for MCX-209."

"Yes," Ulysses confirmed with a shrug. "Penny liked to be involved in a number of high-profile projects. Unfortunately, ultimately, MCX-209 was a failure, as I'm sure you are already aware."

"I'm aware it failed as a cure for Alzheimer's," Holden said. "But something tells me Penny knew it would be because she was a brilliant scientist beneath that socialite veneer." Ulysses remained silent. "Nothing?"

"It wasn't my project. I have little working knowledge of the trials." Ulysses clasped his hands in front of him.

"Then perhaps we can speak with Dr. Odgers's direct supervisor?" Jane prompted.

"Tragically, her supervisor was killed in a freak accident. We were all very saddened by his death. Hector Olonzo was a valuable member of the Tessara family."

"He's dead?" she questioned, finding that way too convenient. Alarm bells clanged loudly in her head. "What kind of freak accident?"

"It was all very tragic. A mugging gone wrong. The man panicked and shot poor Hector as he was leaving his favorite restaurant on Laurel Avenue. Left him dead in the street. Fortunately, from what I understand, Hector, God rest his soul, didn't suffer. Died instantly."

And dead men tell no tales. She shared a look with Holden. "We'd like to take a look at the project files associated with MCX-209," Holden said.

"Again, sorry to disappoint, but due to the sensitive nature of the drug, the Defense Intelligence Department felt it prudent to remove all traces of the drug trials and research from the facility."

Jane nodded remembering something to that effect from Dr. Kat Odgers, Jake Isaac's wife. They could enlist her help to find the missing research. "Penny

Winslow's influence on any project, given the discovery that she was abusing her authority, is immediately suspect," he told Ulysses. "Were you aware of Penny's extracurricular activities outside of this lab?"

"I'm not sure what you're asking," he said calmly.

"I don't believe I need to spell it out," Holden said. "You're a smart man."

"I was unaware of Penny's involvement with I.D.," Ulysses answered, short and sweet and giving away nothing.

Jane glanced at Holden, signaling they were done. The secrets in this building could fill a space station. Whatever Ulysses was protecting, he wouldn't share without a court order to compel him.

"We'll be in touch," she said.

"Good luck in your investigation. As always, Tessara strives to be accommodating."

Did he mean that? Likely not. They were probably having a shredding party this very second, if they hadn't already.

After they left the building and headed to their car, Holden said, "Well, that wasn't entirely a bust. Do you think Hector was killed and it was framed as a tragic mishap?"

"My instincts say yes," Jane said, climbing into the car. She checked her watch. "We'd better hustle if we want to catch our rescheduled flight. I'm ready to put California in my rearview mirror."

Holden agreed. They'd learned everything they were going to learn in this place. Besides, more answers awaited them back in Washington when they hit up Kat Odgers for information on MCX-209.

Once on the plane, buckled in and ready for take-off, Holden asked Jane, "What do you think that winery has to do with all of this? Seemed kind of random."

She nodded. "Maybe we ought to pay a visit and see what shakes out?"

"Definitely. Put it on the list."

"What vibe are you getting from Rocha?" Jane asked.

"Not sure. He's definitely not happy that we're poking around, but I can't tell if it's because he's protecting his investments or because he truly has stuff to hide."

"Same. He hasn't been overtly helpful. Then again, he hasn't refused anything we've asked for, either. He could've made it more difficult to procure those personnel files, but he handed them over with minimal fuss."

"He's pretty tight-lipped about what he knew about Penny's exploits, though. Something tells me he's not quite as innocent as he wants us to think he is."

"Maybe."

A beat of silence followed before Holden said, "Watching you in action is pretty hot."

She sucked in a quick breath and shot him a warning look. "Stop that. We can't be talking like that once we get back to Washington."

"I know," he said, withdrawing with slightly ruffled feathers. Did she have to be so rigid all the time?

"I was just saying…I don't know, I read somewhere that women like to hear that stuff."

"Well, I'm not like most women."

Amen to that. It was one of the reasons he couldn't stop thinking about her. "Roger that," he said, deliberately closing his eyes. "I'm going to catch a few Zs. Some wildcat kept me up all night." He smiled to himself when he heard her gasp in embarrassed indignation. *That's right, babe. Good luck shelving that experience.* He'd liked knowing how to push her buttons before, but now? He knew all the *right* buttons to push to make her squirm—and that was information worth dying for.

Chapter 15

It was late by the time they flew into Washington, and, stubborn woman that she was, Jane insisted on driving home instead of crashing at his place. He tried not to be annoyed because he had no right to be, but when he woke the next morning he was less than refreshed. He'd reopened Pandora's Box and he wanted more. In the brief time they'd dated, he'd enjoyed going to sleep and waking up with Jane, which had been something of a change of pace for him because he never invited women to his apartment. Now he was missing the feel of her warm body next to his, and there was nothing he could do about it. She was determined to be bullheaded. A knock at his front door made him realize not only had he lost out on good REM, he'd overslept, too. He opened the front door and let Jane in with a mumbled good morning in between a big yawn.

"You look like hell," she observed, going to the coffeepot to pour herself a cup. "Still jet-lagged?"

If he looked jet-lagged, she was the exact opposite— she looked as fresh as a daisy. Of course, that rubbed him wrong, too. Why wasn't she suffering like he was? "I'm fine. There's nothing like having the whole bed to yourself."

She nodded. "Sometimes a California King just isn't big enough," she said with a bright smile. Damn, she was good at this game. "You better shower because we have an appointment at Butterfly Bend in an hour and it's at least a 45-minute drive from here."

He swore under his breath, then burned his tongue with hot coffee. "You couldn't have made an afternoon appointment? Jeez, Fallon, give a guy a chance to recover."

"No rest for the wicked, right?"

He had no response. Frankly, he didn't trust himself not to be rude. Maybe a shower would do him some good. Except when he stood under the spray he couldn't help but remember the last shower he shared with Jane, and suddenly it was hard to focus on anything aside from his raging erection. He pushed at his shaft, irritated. Nothing was gonna happen there. *Down, boy.* Think of baseball, grandmothers or the fact that Jane wasn't the least bit interested in picking up where they'd left off. Yeah, that ought to be a good-enough libido killer. He scrubbed down and got out of the shower. Taking little time to dress, he reappeared, hair wet but ready to work.

"You take a longer shower that most girls I know," Jane said, frowning. "What did you do in there, shave your legs?" She grabbed her keys and gestured. "Let's go. We're losing time."

"And you think you're driving?" he asked, incredulously. "If we're going to get there on time, I'd better drive."

Jane was such a stickler for the rules that she stuck religiously to the speed limit. He, on the other hand, treated each destination as a finish line. But Jane wasn't about to budge.

"I would like to arrive alive. How you even have a license is beyond me."

Holden had no choice but to follow. The only consolation was the nice view of Fallon's backside as they left his building. "So you really slept good last night?" he asked.

"Like a baby."

Like a baby, he mimicked in his head as he climbed into the car. Of course she had. Holden punched the address in the GPS and they were on their way. Jane's sensible Honda Accord was exactly the kind of car he'd imagined Jane would drive. It got good gas mileage, was luxurious to a point, but not overly so, and had a sensible price point. He chuckled at his own observation, which caused her to look at him sharply.

"What was that for?"

"Nothing. I was just thinking this car suits you."

She relaxed. "Yeah? It's a good car. *Consumer Re-*

ports lists it as one of the most reliable cars in its class."

"I bet it does." He smirked. "Let me guess…top speed is eighty miles per hour."

"Not that I would need to drive eighty for any reason—we're not on an autobahn. It does have a V6, you know. But why would I need to drive faster than the speed limit? Do you think I have a death wish?"

He barked a laugh. "Jane, live a little, why don't you? There's a whole world waiting for you when you decide to go crazy."

"You can keep crazy. I prefer stability and reliability."

He winced. "Are you a granny? And how is it that you work for the federal government with your low tolerance for risk?"

"Can we talk about something other than personal things? Let's talk about the case," she suggested almost desperately. "I was thinking last night when I couldn't fall asleep that there has to be a connection between Trevor and Penny other than being cousins. The fact that Miko referenced the winery tells me there's something there because why else would Miko mention something so obscure?"

"I thought you said you slept like a baby," he reminded her, latching on to the one thing that mattered to him at the moment. "Maybe you should've stayed with me like I suggested."

"Do you seriously have a one-track mind? Can we please stay on topic?"

He sighed, annoyed he was so easily pushed aside.

"Yeah, sure. I was just saying that, you know, it might have been nice.... Forget it."

"I told you we can't do what we did in California. You and I both know it's a huge mistake, and I'm not doing anything to jeopardize this case. I'm surprised you're fighting me on this. Why are you so hurt that I don't want a relationship with you?"

"Hurt? Who said I'm hurt?" he repeated, indignant. "You're right—we should just stick to the case."

"Thank you. Now you're making sense. All right, so here's the deal—I say we question this Trevor Granger and find out why Miko would've been aware of Trevor and Penny's relationship. And in the meantime, I wonder if we could get James to do some more poking around."

"Such as?"

"Such as taking a look around the Department of Defense and see if they are holding on to anything beyond our pay grade."

Holden whistled in appreciation. "I take it back. You do like to live dangerously. So you're saying we should set James on the trail that might lead to the Department of Defense's doorstep? Essentially hacking into a government mainframe? That might take more than twenty grand. Are you footing this bill?"

"He might be willing to do it just for fun. His type love the opportunity to hack into government mainframes. It's like a badge of honor," she said. "But I guess we can wait and see what we find out on our own before we tap that resource."

"It's worth keeping in our pocket for plan B,"

Holden said, eyeing her with deeper appreciation, not only for her sexy body, but also for her incredibly sexy brain. He angled himself toward her. "Listen, I know we said we wouldn't talk about personal stuff, but you have to admit there's still a spark between us."

"Obviously. That's not the point, though. Neither one of us is suited for a relationship with the other. Why complicate matters when there's no need?"

"Maybe I like complicated."

She made an exasperated noise. "That's the problem—I don't. It's just easier to keep things professional between us."

"Easy is boring. And you don't want boring. You're the kind of woman who needs a challenge or else you stagnate in your own rigid personality. My guess is before your dad made you dance to his tune, you were less buttoned-down."

"What makes you say that?"

"Because I've seen your wild side, and there's no way that sexy woman came out of nowhere. She's just been on lockdown for far too long."

Jane risked a small smile, but she smothered it quickly enough to drop a bomb on him. "Listen, I didn't want to do this, but the bottom line is this— you'll never be good enough in the eyes of my family. Even before this situation with Miko blew up, you had no cred with my dad. He has a certain standard, and you don't live up to it. I'm sorry. It's harsh, but those are the facts. I'm not going to spend my entire life defending you against my family or fighting with family over you."

Ouch. He felt as if she'd just delivered a round-house kick to his nuts. And what the hell? He wasn't good enough? How much more cred did he need? "Last time I checked I was a pretty good catch," he told her, his temper rising. "Highly decorated marine, level VI security clearance in the CIA and built like a Mack truck. I don't see the problem."

"I love your enthusiasm and confidence, but it has nothing to do with your qualifications *per se.* It has everything to do with the way my family perceives you."

"I'm confused. Are you saying it's not me, it's your family?"

"Sort of."

"Oh, good. For a second I thought you were throwing up imaginary obstacles." He rolled his eyes as his voice dripped with sarcasm. Unbelievable. He was considered a good catch by most standards. Except to the one person he wanted to impress, for some stupid reason. "Listen, just admit to me that you and I shared something pretty incredible, and I'll leave it at that."

"You'll drop it?"

"Sure," he lied. Drop it? He was going to gnaw on that sucker like a dog with a bone. But his ego demanded she tell the truth. "Just admit I rocked your world and we'll go back to being simply partners without benefits."

She drew a deep breath and blew it out in a long exhale. "Okay, Holden. We have chemistry. Real, visceral, unexplainable chemistry, and this weekend was a brutal reminder that we are desperately good together. Is that what you want to hear? Well, I'll do you a solid and go a step further. The reason I couldn't sleep last night was because I was thinking of what we did together and how I already missed the feeling of you beside me. It that enough? Does that help? Because frankly, I think it makes it worse."

The tight band of tension cording his chest loosened and he could actually breathe again. As long as she was fighting the same fight he was, there was a chance. A chance at what, he wasn't sure, but he wanted to find out. "Yeah, it'll do." He didn't even try to smother the grin. "Now, tell me again why we shouldn't be partners with benefits?"

"You're impossible," she growled, and shot him an extremely irritated look. She switched on the radio and effectively shut him out. "From now on, no more talking."

What was his problem? Why did he care what her family thought of him? Jane was baffled by Holden's reaction, but even more so by the pinch she felt in her conscience for hurting his feelings. They'd shared a whirlwind of good times until it'd come grinding to a halt, which had been the wake-up call she had needed to put her head back on straight. The memory of ending it popped into her mind as she drove, and she lingered a little too long, because within seconds she was back in that wretched moment.

"What do you mean, you're ending things?" Holden had demanded to know, standing apart from her, pissed as hell and more than a little hurt. "This is crap and you know it. Everything was going fine until your dad got involved."

"And who got him involved?" she had shot back, still mad at him for thinking he knew how to handle the situation with her father better than her. "I told you to back off, but you refused and did whatever you thought was necessary and it blew up in our faces. Well, congrats—this is your reward!"

"You're punishing me for trying to talk to your dad for *us?*" he'd asked with open incredulity. "That's rich, Fallon. Totally rich. Remind me never to do you a solid ever again."

"Oh, don't try to delude yourself into thinking you did that for me. It was all about you. The charming Holden Archangelo thought he could bamboozle my father into liking him and it went sour. End of story."

"Believe what you want, but I did it for *you!* It's not natural for you to live under your father's thumb for the rest of your life. For crying out loud, Fallon, you're still balancing his damn checkbook!"

"There's nothing wrong with that," she'd said stubbornly, though she had tried to talk her father into hiring an accountant. The Major had shut her down pretty quickly, saying he couldn't trust strangers with his finances. Then when she'd tried to enlist the help of her brothers, The Major had shut her down on that score, too, saying Ian and Walker were too busy to handle an extra assignment. "If you were close to your father, Holden, you'd understand. My dad needs me and I enjoy being able to help."

"No, you crave that tiny pat on the head that he

doles out like a miser with his gold," Holden had returned, and her cheeks had burned with the insult because it was partly true. Even though she was overloaded with responsibilities, it gave her a small amount of pleasure knowing her father valued her help in this one way. He still managed to find fault each time, which always put a damper on the meager amount of satisfaction she received for the work. Holden must've peeked inside her brain because he'd then said, "See? Even you know it's true. When are you going to start living your life for you instead of everyone else? What about your brothers? Do they beg for your father's approval before they date someone?"

"No," she'd answered, her cheeks burning even hotter. "My dad doesn't seem to care who they date."

"Why? Because somehow they're perfect judges of character? And if that's so, why can't they trust your judgment?"

"Stop it!" She'd clapped her hands over her ears, unable to listen to another minute of Holden punching holes in her life. Everything he'd said rang with truth, but she hadn't been ready to burn down the house just because the roof leaked a little. "I don't tell you how to be with your family, so shut the hell up. I don't even know why you're so upset about my ending things. I thought you were the perennial bachelor? This should be a blessing. You ought to be thanking me for letting you off the hook. I mean, c'mon, Holden, what did you think? That we were going to run off and get married or something? We were just sleeping together. That's it. And now it's over."

Holden had held her stare, his mouth a tight line of frustrated anger, but there had been hurt in his eyes. It had been the secret pain he was trying to hide that had twisted her heart. She'd done that. She'd put that look in his eyes. And a part of her mourned her own actions, but if her father had taught her anything, it was how to make the hard choice with a stiff upper lip. *Thanks, Dad.*

"So you really didn't sleep well last night," Holden asked, breaking into her thoughts. She was so grateful to be out of her own head that she answered truthfully.

"Yeah, too many memories. Both good and bad," she admitted. "I feel as if I only got a few winks. Reminds me of when I was stationed in Iraq. That was a bloody awful time."

"Iraq is a dusty bowl of insurgent nightmares. I spent a tour there. Then I got shipped off to Afghanistan for another crap detail that nearly got my ass shot off."

She smiled in weary commiseration. "It feels like that. I swear I have sand in my eyes." He reached over and massaged the back of her neck, gently squeezing the muscles holding up her head, and she groaned. "That felt awesome," she said with a sigh, just for a moment enjoying the simple pleasure. Jane cast Holden a brief smile and he smiled back, igniting tiny bubbles in her stomach. She shook her head.

"You're a hard habit to break," she murmured, mostly to herself, but Holden heard and chuckled.

"Glad to hear it. Soothes my bruised ego a little."

Funny how the little sleep she'd managed with Holden had been wholly satisfying, yet the eight hours she had supposedly gotten last night made her feel as if she'd slept only two winks. She refused to believe it was anything more than wild, crazy attraction between two people who were turned on by the forbidden aspect of their relationship. What other option was there? Was she falling in love with Holden? Goodness gracious, she hoped not. She didn't need that complication. Maybe it wasn't love but simply the draw of a forbidden relationship. Maybe she was a bit of a bad girl. Maybe a latent naughtiness inside of her was spurring her to do things outside of her nature. That must be the answer, because ever since Holden had been thrown into her life, she'd been doing and saying things that were so far afield of what she would ever say or do she almost didn't recognize herself. The weird part? She kind of liked it. She liked this feeling of having no rules, or better yet, saying screw the rules and just going for it. Her grip tightened on the steering wheel. Yes, sometimes rule breaking was fun. Especially if it was with Holden. But right now they had a case to figure out. And she had a feeling they were only scratching the surface of something really bad.

Chapter 16

They pulled off the highway and found themselves on a long winding road that carved through the scenic mountainside cloaked in the bitter cold of winter. "It's a little creepy, yet beautiful at the same time," she observed. "I've never actually heard of a winery in Washington. Aren't most wineries in California?"

"Your guess is as good as mine. I'm not exactly a wine drinker. I prefer beer myself."

"Me, too."

Holden flashed her a grin as they pulled into the winery parking lot. "All right, let's see what this winery dude has to tell us," he said as they climbed from the car.

An imposing rock-and-brick building rose from the ground, the design both old world and modern at the same time. An affluent stamp marked the property; everywhere they looked the evidence of big money stared back. Rolling hills lined with rows upon rows of gnarled grape vines lashed to rigging to keep them upright went as far as the eye could see. Snow dotted the mountaintops above them. It was romantic and breathtakingly scenic. Too bad they weren't out sightseeing.

An older man with a sharp smile emerged from the house and quickly introduced himself. "You must be Agent Archangelo and Agent Fallon. Nice to meet you. My name is Trevor Granger. I own Butterfly Bend."

"Thank you for agreeing to see us on such short notice," Jane said.

"No problem. We're off season right now, so things slow to an acceptable pace around here. Now, if this meeting had happened in September, I would've had to tell you to take a number." He laughed at his own joke and Jane and Holden simply smiled politely as they followed him into the warmth of the building. Inside was just as lovely as the outside. Tastefully decorated with an understated wealth, it looked as if a set decorator had dressed it for a scene. "Can I get you some coffee or fresh scones?" he offered. A scone tempted Jane, but she declined, as did Holden. However, the man wouldn't take no for an answer. "Are you sure? Fresh from the oven. There is nothing better than a fresh scone with homemade cream. And don't even try to let anyone tell you the stuff in the can is just as good as cream whipped to a perfect peak. Lies, I tell you. It's the real deal or nothing."

"I agree, sir." Holden smiled. "Maybe I will take one of those scones."

Trevor snapped his fingers and a round dark-haired woman appeared from the kitchen carrying a tray. Her graying hair sprang from her head in unruly strands, and a warm smile wreathed her mouth as she offered the plate for his selection. "Maria is the best baker in all of Washington. I know this because she used to run her own bakery and I made her an offer she couldn't refuse. Now she bakes for me."

Jane looked to Maria, surprised. "You gave up your business to be the baker for Mr. Granger?"

Maria bobbed her head. "Oh, yes. Mr. Granger is very generous. And I love working here."

Trevor nodded at Maria's answer and then she scuttled off. "I always say treat your hired help well and you'll never be left with open positions," he shared with a patronizing smile. "Maria has been with us for two years now and it's because of her my waistline is getting a little bit thicker. I don't mind, though."

Holden groaned as he enjoyed his bite. "Whatever her salary is, she's worth it. This is the most amazing scone I've ever had in my life."

Jane startled when he pushed a scone at her. "No, thank you," she said in a low tone, annoyed that Holden was so easily distracted. Honestly, how did this man ever get anything done? She looked to Trevor. "Mr. Granger, you might wonder why we called this meeting today. We have some questions regarding your cousin, Penny Winslow, or as you knew her, Penelope Granger. Did you have anything to do with a company called Tessara?"

"Oh, yes. Penelope was helping me develop a new type of cork for my wine bottles. One of the problems that we have is cork disintegration over time. She was helping me create a coating that would go over the cork and prevent it from disintegrating without affecting the integrity of the wine."

"Why not just use plastic?" Jane suggested.

"My dear, one does not simply use plastic in the wine that has been selected as the Presidential Reserve. Plastic has chemicals that affect the wine's integrity. My reputation would be ruined if I dared to use a plastic cork."

"Oh," Jane said, not meaning to offend the man. "So was she successful?"

"Yes, she was. I received a shipment of the new corks last month. Unfortunately, Penelope is not here to celebrate with me. We were very close and her death took a toll on my health. I still get choked up when I let myself dwell. She was a tremendous woman and like a sister to me."

"I'm sorry for your loss," Jane murmured, but from what she had read, Penny Winslow was a sociopath. Her death was a blessing; however, this man had been her family, so Jane would try to be respectful. "It may grieve you to learn that Penny was involved in a number of illegal activities."

"I recall some of the more sordid newspaper headlines," Trevor said, his mouth pinching in a disgusted moue. "But I've come to realize the truth doesn't always make for the best headline. I choose not to believe such lies about my cousin. She was a generous woman who believed in volunteering and was involved in various humanitarian works. Surely you've read some of the many articles about her charitable giving? I'd hate to think that all my cousin Penny will be remembered for is the lies that were printed about her toward the end of her life."

"Penny was found guilty by the law—those were not lies," Holden said. "I'm sorry to be the bearer of bad news. I'm sure she was a different person with you."

Trevor jerked a short nod but kept his lips tight, which Jane had to respect. Sometimes it was hard to remember that even bad people were loved by someone.

"That's what brings us here today," Holden continued. "It seems Penny was involved with more than just good works."

"Such as capitalism," Jane murmured, unable to stop herself. Holden cast her a look, and she buttoned up. She knew that comments like that weren't exactly helpful. Thankfully, it didn't appear as if Trevor had caught her muttered dig.

"I don't want to tarnish the memory of your cousin, but the person she was to you isn't the person she was to everyone. Penny was abusing her position for personal gain. Again, I'm sorry to pour salt in the wound, but we need to know why my brother, Miko, would've mentioned your winery in covert notebooks that also involve your cousin Penny. Do you have any idea why he would have mentioned Butterfly Bend?"

Trevor shook his head with a faint frown. "I haven't a clue. I assure you, nothing illegal is happening on these premises. I have too much to lose to mess with anything that might cost me my livelihood. You don't get selected to create the Presidential Reserve without keeping your nose clean."

"What is the Presidential Reserve?" Jane asked. He'd mentioned it twice now, so it must be important.

"We were tasked to create an original blend specifically for the White House. Any event is served with a white and red of Butterfly Bend Presidential Reserve."

"Wow. That's quite a coup," Holden said, and Trevor nodded.

"See? I wouldn't risk everything I have for anyone, not even my beloved cousin."

"How does one earn the designation of the Presidential Reserve?" Holden asked.

"Cultivating the right connections along with creating award-winning wines is essential."

"And you obviously managed both criteria."

"For two years running now," Trevor said, puffing out his chest with pride. "In fact, we're shipping another batch of wine at the end of this month for a special presidential dinner. It's a small gathering, not the usual five hundred head count, just the executive branch."

"Nice," Holden said, holding a brief smile, but Jane could feel the frustration starting to roll off him that not even a delicious scone could divert. They were at another dead end. Trevor Granger didn't give off a criminal vibe, and they couldn't go after a guy simply because he had crappy relatives. "Thank you for your help. I think we've taken up enough of your time."

Trevor rose as they did, looking eager to please again. "I'm happy to be of service to the government in any way I can."

Yes, so keep those kickbacks flowing my way, Jane thought derisively as her smile remained fixed. "We'll be in touch if there's anything else we need."

Trevor saw them outside, then Jane and Holden put Butterfly Bend in their rearview mirror. "I really thought that was going to lead somewhere," Jane said once they hit the freeway. Holden's disappointment was tangible and squeezing out the air in the car. "Tomorrow we'll check out that safety deposit box," she said, trying to lift his spirits. "Something helpful is bound to be in that. I can feel it in my bones."

He graced her with a short smile to acknowledge her but otherwise remained silent the entire ride back to his place. But as they exited the car, Holden stopped her to ask, "How about dinner?" and she knew the smart thing to do would be to politely decline, but his vulnerable expression tugged at her in a way that, if she'd been thinking clearly, would've been a warning.

"Just dinner?"

"Sure."

"I don't believe you," she said bluntly.

"And would it be so bad if it turned out to be more than just dinner?"

She sighed. "Yes and no."

"Is it mostly yes or mostly no?"

"I think it's mostly freezing out here. Promise me it'll just be dinner and we'll talk about the case, and I'll stay."

With a look of resignation, he agreed. "Sure. A working dinner. Sounds great."

Oh, he's lying through his perfect teeth. He wants more and he'll try to get it, too. And yet... "All right. What's for dinner?"

"I have a few steaks in the fridge. How are you with a salad?"

She cast a derisive look his way as they entered the building. "I can make a salad that'll knock your socks off. Remember? Even my father, who is as persnickety as it comes, raves about my salads."

"Good." He smirked and started climbing the stairs, giving her an excellent view of his beautiful butt.

Yeah...this was so not a good idea.

Holden was trying not to let his disappointment color the evening, but it was there, beneath the surface, lurking like an unwelcome guest, sullying his enjoyment of a decent evening with Jane. By the time the wine came out, he was ready to talk.

"So how long are you going to pretend like everything is okay?" she asked as they walked to the living room and sat on the sofa together. It felt intimate as the fire crackled in the gas grate and filled the room with dancing light. Dinner had been fantastic. Between his grilling skills and Jane's epic salad-making talents, they'd made a dinner worth talking about. Jane tucked her feet beneath her and faced him as she sipped her wine. "I get it…I was hoping for more to go off, too."

He stared at his wine, wishing he'd grabbed a beer, but he took a measured sip anyway before answering. "The clock is ticking. I needed there to be more to go off. The end of the week is approaching fast. Going to California ate up valuable time."

"Chief Harris will give us more time if we can show him what we've got."

"What do we have? A bunch of uncomfortable coincidences? A few plausible theories? Which translate to nothing that will stand up in court. I can't let this go, Jane. Why couldn't Miko have left behind less cryptic clues?" he asked with frustration.

"You miss him." It was a statement, not a question. Of course he missed him, but he sensed she knew that it went deeper than that. And she was right.

"Miko and I were always close. Goes with the twin territory. But I think because our old man was such a sorry excuse for a father we leaned on each other even more than most brothers would. We were each other's support system. We did everything together."

"From the limited information I know about twins, that sounds about right. What changed?"

"Miko changed. That last year he was standoffish and started pushing me away. He became surly and curt whenever I tried to find out what was wrong. By the time he died, we were barely speaking. Sometimes I wonder if that's why he did it—he didn't know how to reach out to me anymore."

"That must've been hard for you, not having your brother around like you used to."

"It was hell. I tried to blow it off, but it was there, sticking in my throat like a chicken bone, choking me to death. And there was nothing I could do about it. Miko was determined to keep me at arm's length. Now I kick myself for not pushing harder for answers."

"Before this investigation with you, I would've said he was reacting to a guilty conscience." She swirled her wine. "Now I think there might be some merit to the theory he was protecting you."

He thanked her with a smile. "Well, I sure hope so. Then again, I wish he would've just told me what was going on. I might've been able to help and maybe he'd still be here."

She nodded and sipped from her glass. They sat in easy, comfortable silence, and Holden wondered if he'd ever felt more at ease with a woman, much less one he'd slept with. He'd never been one for long-term attachments, but he liked the idea of attaching to Jane. Something about her turned his crank in all the right ways. Hell, even the way she stubbornly refused to be with him because of her father and brothers—that dogged loyalty—was sexy. "You close with your brothers?" he asked.

Jane took her time answering, as if she didn't

want to inadvertently say something that would reflect badly on her family. "Yeah, they're good guys.
Sometimes I wish they'd stop mirroring our father
and stop treating me like some fragile female who
can't parallel park. Frankly, I pity the women they
end up with. Impossible standards."

He chuckled at this rare bit of sharing. Must be
the wine loosening her tongue. "So they've never
brought home a special woman? Someone they were
in a long-term relationship with?"

"No. I don't think either of them are interested in
settling down. Sometimes I think my mom did a number on all of us. Fear of commitment seems a pretty
common theme among the Fallon men."

"So that's why your dad never remarried?"

"I guess." A wry smile lifted her lips. "But what
woman would put up with him? Aside from Claudine,
of course. And even then…sometimes I wish she'd
just whack him upside the head."

"Whoa…look at you, feeling your oats," Holden
said, smiling. "And who is Claudine?"

"My dad's housekeeper and cook. She keeps him
looking civilized. Heaven forbid he leave the house
without his shirts perfectly pressed. Until Claudine
came around, I was expected to handle that detail.
To this day, I hate ironing," she revealed. "I send out
my clothes to a dry cleaner. I'm not even sure I own
an iron."

He laughed. "Feels good, huh? Breaking the
rules?"

She shared his laughter. "Yeah. When I got my

first apartment, I ate straight from the peanut-butter jar, just stuck my finger in and took a dollop. My father would've had a heart attack if he'd seen me do that at home."

"My old man used to keep his fishing gear in the garage and never, under any circumstances, were we allowed to touch it. Well, he was drunk more often than he was sober and when the hell was he going to go fishing? So during the summer Miko and I would grab his gear and go down to the creek whenever he passed out. We'd catch a few fish, grill 'em up out in the woods, then come home with full bellies and the old man snoring off his bender, none the wiser. That is, until Miko broke the rod."

"Oh, damn. How'd you get out of that one?"

"We convinced the old man he'd broken it during one of his drunken rages. He couldn't ever remember what he did during those times, so he bought it. Saved our asses, I can tell you that."

Their shared laughter wove a tighter band of closeness around them, and it was hard not to feel it pulling them together. "This is nice," she said quietly. "I'm glad you invited me to dinner. You're not half-bad on the grill."

"And you're not half-bad with the greens."

"Not a bad team, I guess."

"Not bad at all."

Holden withheld the sigh building behind his chest. She was so beautiful. He could stare at her all night— and not in a creeper sort of way, but in an *I think I love you sort of way.* He couldn't tell her that yet.

That was a shortcut to losing all the good feelings between them. Wasn't that his dumb luck? *Find a good woman that you can't have. Good going, Archangelo.* Time to switch things up a bit before he sank too low into his own maudlin thoughts. "Tell me about growing up with The Major," he said. "I can imagine, but paint me a picture."

She groaned. "That's a boring picture and you've already painted a pretty accurate version."

"Humor me."

"Fine." She sighed, settling her empty glass on the coffee table. "Well, it was as you imagined: Very strict, very regimented and little room for dissent in the ranks. And I was always at the bottom of the chain of command."

"Is it because you were the youngest?"

"No. It was because I was a female."

"Your father is sexist?"

"Oh, in the worst way, and he doesn't even apologize for it. Men are smarter, more capable and more trustworthy—according to The Major."

"Ouch. But you're highly accomplished," he pointed out, really fighting the urge to tell Jane that her father was a card-carrying asshole.

"Yeah, and you'd think I'd get an *atta boy* now and then, but nope. I'm successful *because* of my father. He's flat-out told me the reason I've risen in the ranks is because of who my father is."

"That's total bullshit. I've seen your file."

She cocked a brow at him. "Oh? A little light reading?"

"If you've seen your file you know it's not light reading. You've got some serious cred behind your name, and it's not because of your father. You know, Jane, just because someone is serving up cow manure doesn't mean you have to take a bite."

A warm, vulnerable sweetness suffused her expression and he wondered if she knew just how fabulous she was. She was the total package: beauty, brawn and brains. Any guy would be lucky to call her his. And The Major was an idiot for not realizing what a treasure his daughter was. "You can be pretty charming when you put your mind to it," she said.

"I know," he grinned, placing his wineglass near hers and leaning toward her to steal a kiss. She stopped him with a gentle hand, her gaze searching his. "Let me kiss you," he said softly, but she shook her head in a small motion. "Why not?"

"You know why."

"Do you want me to kiss you?" he said, startling her with his abrupt change in tactic. She worried her bottom lip, almost in invitation, and when she slowly nodded, his smile deepened as he closed the distance between their lips. "Then let me."

Chapter 17

Jane allowed Holden to press her into the soft cushion as his mouth teased hers in a brutally devastating invasion that left her aching and wanting. The spiraling need drilling down to her groin flushed her system with hazy desire and she clung to Holden, needing to feel him against her. What was it about this man that sent her good sense running for cover? It wasn't that he was simply a good lover—she'd enjoyed plenty of men between the sheets—so what was it? Something about Holden called out to that distinctly feminine part of herself and caused it to go weak in the knees with butterfly wings in the belly. Talk about an occupational hazard.

"You are the most sensual woman I've ever met," he said against her lips, helping her out of her sweater and tossing it aside. He ran his fingers along the lacy cups of her bra and then nuzzled the valley of her breasts, inhaling her scent. "And your skin smells like cake and cookies." He sat up suddenly to ask, "Why is that, exactly?"

"Brown Sugar and Brownie body lotion," she answered with an embarrassed laugh. "I bought it on a whim."

"Well, it's amazing," he growled, moving to her neck. "As if you weren't delicious enough…."

She laughed with pure delight as he teased all the sensitive spots of her neck, sucking and biting until she was no longer laughing but panting and pulling at the buckle on his jeans. "So impatient," he chuckled as he leaned back to give her better access.

She pinned him with a sensual look as she made quick work of his jeans and shoved them down around his thighs. "If we're going to go balls to the wall with career-ending moves, we'd better make it worth our while."

"Hell yeah, baby," he agreed feverishly, sucking in a tight breath when her lips wrapped around the head of his erection. Jane thrilled at the way the backs of his knees trembled as she worked him with her mouth. His fingers threaded through her hair and pulled with delectable pressure. He guided her with his hands, his touch becoming urgent. "Oh, jeez, Janey…oh!" He tried to push her away, but she wasn't going to let him. She wanted him to know that she gave as good as she got and she expected his best. She wanted him to forget about Miko for tonight and just enjoy being in the company of a woman. His moan turned her on as much as his kisses. She rose and planted a kiss on his mouth before leading him to his bedroom. "Marry me, Jane Fallon," he said breathlessly as he tumbled to the bed, grinning like the devil as she straddled him. "You've just ruined me for other women."

"Too bad for you," she teased as she wiggled on top of him, taunting him with her body. "Now it's your turn. Whaddya got for me?"

His playful demeanor changed, and with a growl he rolled her onto her back so he towered over her. She knew that look and it thrilled her senseless. She felt stripped bare, as if he could see into her very soul, and although it was a foreign sensation, with Holden she wasn't afraid. "You shouldn't throw down gauntlets like that, sweet girl," he warned in a silky tone as he plucked at a puckered nipple with his lips. She shuddered and grinned. He was such a tease. "Now there will be no mercy."

"Bring it on," she dared, lifting her chin with a smile. "I can take whatever you can dish out."

One dark brow lifted as a slow, sexy smile formed on his lips, making her shiver in anticipation as he said, "Challenge accepted," right before sealing his mouth to hers in a mind-altering kiss.

As Holden moved between her legs, she clamped a hand over her eyes as she lost herself in pure pleasure and realized it was official—she was addicted to Holden Archangelo.

And just like all good addictions, he had the power to trash everything she'd worked so hard for in her life.

Holden awoke to the feel of Jane trying to stealthily climb from his bed. "Where are you going?" he asked groggily, rubbing his mouth and trying to focus his vision.

"Home."

The one-word answer made him roll his eyes. He was too tired to argue with her even though he thought she was being ridiculous. If she wanted to bail, sneaking out the door like a one-night stand, so be it. He wasn't going to stop her.

Yeah, that lasted about a minute. He jumped from the bed and followed her to the living room, where she was trying to collect her strewn clothing. "What are you doing, aside from being irritatingly stubborn?"

She straightened, and even in the moonlight he could see the flash in her eyes at his insult. "I never told you I would stay. I don't do that."

"Well, newsflash, I don't, either. Consider it an honor I want you to stay."

"Can you hear yourself? An honor? Get over yourself, Holden. Maybe it isn't about you. Ever think of that? I knew this was a mistake and I never should've let my emotions make the call." She pulled her sweater over her head and jerked on her jeans. "But trust me, it won't happen again. I'm not your partner with benefits. Got it?"

"Loud and clear, honey."

"Good. Then we won't have to ever revisit this conversation." She grabbed her purse, and seconds later she was gone.

Like a bullet exiting the chamber.

He swore under his breath and padded back to his bedroom, shutting the door and climbing back into bed. *Women—they were all crazy.*

Even ones who look stable.

Jane's fingers shook as she slipped her key into her front door. What was wrong with her? Had she no self-will? Holden was like a secret weapon, able to destroy a woman's defenses with one charming twist of his lips, and that wasn't even talking about once he had her on her back.

She walked into her living room and headed straight for her answering machine. Even though it was two in the morning, she couldn't ignore the blinking light of a waiting message. She yawned and pressed play. The nasally voice of a telemarketer followed and she quickly hit Delete. The second message started to play, but she heard nothing but dead air. She frowned and deleted. "No more messages" was the green light giving her permission to find her bed. She started to pull off her sweater and toss it into the laundry basket when something caught her eye. Just as she bent to investigate what turned out to be a coin on the carpet, the sharp tinkle of busting glass startled the drowsiness out of her and she dropped to the floor, her heart pounding. Broken glass littered the floor and cold, outside air seeped in from the small, bullet-shaped hole in her master bedroom window. Someone had been waiting for her. If she hadn't seen the penny on the floor, she'd be sporting metal in the back of her skull. She swallowed and closed her eyes, willing her heart rate to slow down. They might still be out there. She rolled away and slowly stood, her back hugging the wall as she grabbed her gun from the nightstand and crept to the window. She made a quick, peripheral scan and saw nothing but the usual cars parked in her neighborhood. She pulled her cell and quickly dialed Holden. He answered on the second ring. "Calling to apologize?"

"Someone just shot at me through my bedroom window," she whispered.

"Stay where you are," he said, all jocularity gone from his voice. "I'm coming."

"I'm capable of handling myself," she reminded him, and he groaned.

"Damn it, Janey, this isn't some macho attempt at treating you like a little lady who can't handle a crisis. This is about waiting for freaking backup so you don't end up getting killed."

She nodded, realizing he was right. Why else would she have called Holden, right? "Be careful," she said. "There could be more than one shooter out there."

"I'm calling it in. In the meantime, find a defensible spot and stay there."

"I will."

He clicked off and Jane tucked her phone into her pocket before going to her bedroom closet and shutting herself inside. She had a clear view of her bedroom door from the slats, and if anyone tried to follow up on that shot, she'd unload her clip in his or her face. That was a sniper shot, she realized, studying the damage with a critical eye. Chances were they knew they'd missed their mark, and snipers weren't usually the ones charging in for hand-to-hand combat. She double-checked her ammunition and waited, eyes adjusted to the darkness, waiting for anyone who didn't belong there to come busting through her bedroom door. *Go ahead, asshole. Make my day.*

Holden broke about four traffic laws as he nearly topped the speed barrier to get to Jane's. All the while, weaving in and out of traffic, he was on the phone to Reed.

"Someone shot at Jane," he said. "I'm on my way to her place now. Send backup. I don't know how many shooters there are or if they've compromised her house in any other way."

Even though Reed was in his sixties and had likely been fast asleep in dreamland, he snapped to action like a man half his age. "I'll send in a team. Don't worry—it's a team I trust."

"Thanks, Chief."

"Is Jane okay?" he asked.

"She's fine. But this takes it to a whole new level, wouldn't you say? Jane gets shot at after we start poking around in Miko's case?"

"Could be," Reed agreed. "We'll debrief later.

Right now, get to Jane. I want you both in a safe place for the rest of the night."

"I'll take her back to my place," he said. "It's constructed with reinforced steel and bulletproof glass. Ain't nothing getting through that place. I can guarantee it."

"Sounds good. I want a full report at 0800 hours."

Reed clicked off and Holden tossed his phone onto the passenger seat. Within ten minutes, he was at Jane's, and within another ten of his arrival, the cavalry arrived.

A quick but thorough perimeter sweep revealed the shooter had bailed, which didn't surprise Holden. It *did* fill him with impotent rage—he'd wanted to beat him or her to a bloody pulp. He texted Jane that he was coming to the front door, and she met him there. She hadn't changed from when she left his house, and though he had no doubt she could take care of herself, she still looked a bit shaken.

While the team collected forensics, Holden took Jane into the living room. "Tell me exactly what happened."

"There's not much to tell. I came home, I listened to messages and then I went to my bedroom to change for bed. I saw a penny on the floor and bent to retrieve it. That's when the bullet came through the window. Honestly, if the penny hadn't been there, I wouldn't be talking to you right now. That sniper was waiting for me."

Not much to go on. But then if a sniper had been hired to take Jane out, he or she wasn't going to leave tracks for anyone to follow. "Chief said you're to come home with me," he said, expecting and halting her protests with a firm shake of his head. "Your place is compromised and we don't have time to set up a safe house. No arguments—you're coming home with me."

She opened her mouth, then snapped it shut with an almost weary expression and nodded. "Fine. Whatever. I'm exhausted and I need sleep. Your couch is as good as any."

As if. If she wanted to pretend she was going to crash on the couch, so be it. But that wasn't going to happen. He wanted her right beside him. And that was nonnegotiable.

Chapter 18

Jane opened her eyes to the milky morning dawn and listened to Holden's steady breathing. Somehow she'd known she'd end up here, in his bed, but she'd tried to hold out only to cave when he'd simply steered her to the bedroom and started gently removing her clothing. And when he'd simply tucked her in and then climbed in beside her, pulling her to him and holding her tightly, her heart had melted a little. There'd been something so protective, so sweet, about the way he'd known what she had needed, even if she wasn't willing to admit it. She'd slept hard even though she'd only gotten four hours of shut-eye. Someone had tried to kill her. Someone had been lying in wait to end her life. A delicate shudder zinged through her. It'd been a long time since she'd seen active combat, and she'd forgotten how vulnerable it felt to have your life compromised at the drop of a hat.

"Why are you awake?" he asked in a voice husky with sleep. He nuzzled her neck and settled more firmly against her. "You should be sleeping."

"I can't sleep anymore. My mind is racing." At her answer, she sensed that he awoke more fully. She smiled as his breath tickled the back of her neck. "A penny saved my life. What are the odds of that?"

"Pretty damn spectacular. Talk about your lucky penny. I'd hold on to that one."

She nodded, chuckling. "Makes me think I ought to go play the slots or something to take advantage of this lucky streak."

"Now, there's an idea." Holden moved until he was covering her, settling his body along hers, pushing the hair from her eyes and meeting her gaze. "Listen, we're going to find the son of a bitch who tried to kill you, and then we're going to make them wish they'd never been born. Got it?"

She nodded, smiling up at him, loving the feel of his solid body pressing hers. She wrapped her arms around his torso. "I like it when you go all John Wayne," she teased.

"There's plenty more where that came from, missy, *whuha,*" he drawled in a terrible John Wayne imitation, then bending to tease her neck in small, nipping kisses and tickling her until she squealed. "Now how about I show you how a real man wakes up his woman...."

And because he began doing things that made her

eyes roll up into her head with insane pleasure, she forgave him the term *his woman*. But a tiny part of her loved being his woman, even if only for this moment.

"I'm just saying," she teased. "I didn't know guys actually enjoyed foofy coffeehouse drinks." She laughed as they walked into the office, both carrying their respective drinks.

"There's nothing foofy about a chai tea latte," Holden insisted. "Besides, you can laugh all you like. You know you want a taste of my sweet, carefully brewed tea that has been perfectly infused with a splash of vanilla and plenty of fresh whipped cream."

Jane's peal of laughter lit up his soul and almost made him forget that someone had tried to kill her last night, but the reminder crashed into his reality seconds later when he saw a stern older man pacing inside the chief's office, obviously upset and demanding answers. Jane followed his gaze and suddenly her smile froze. "Guess who came to visit," he said, just as unhappy at seeing The Major again as Jane was to know the man was likely giving the chief a ration of shit over last night's event.

She set her cup on her desk and straightened. "Stay here, *please,*" she instructed firmly, halting him in midstep. He wanted to follow, but he sensed that would only make things worse for Jane. The Major looked the same as Holden remembered, and he certainly hadn't changed in his disposition, if his facial expression was anything to go on. He tried not to stare at the man through the glass panel of the chief's office. He'd love to give Jane's father a piece of his mind for being a jackass to his only daughter, but Jane wouldn't appreciate his interference. If he learned anything from the last go-round, it was that Jane prickled when it came to defending her father. He glanced down at himself and immediately straightened his clothing and brushed at stray bits of snow clinging to his suit. Jane had said that The Major wouldn't accept him as a match for his daughter. What a crock of crap. Holden suspected no one would be good enough for The Major's daughter, and if the man weren't such a controlling jackass, that might be an endearing thought by a concerned father. That was not where The Major's motivation was grounded, though.

Everything inside Holden told him to follow her, to not let her face her father alone. He sighed. He knew he was reacting to some primal need to protect when Jane was no weak-willed female. She could probably break something of his without popping a sweat. He grinned in spite of the odd train of his thoughts, but when his gaze returned to Jane and The Major, his smile faded. Whatever was going on in there did not bode well.

He could feel it in his bones.

"My daughter will no longer be part of this investigation," The Major declared, ignoring Jane's gasp of outrage that he should think he had the power to snip careers and make life hell for anyone who dared to naysay him. Maybe he did, but Jane didn't care. She wasn't allowing anyone to push her off this case.

"Stop it! You can't control what cases I investigate." She looked to the chief for backup.

"Let's just take a seat and breathe for a minute," Chief Harris suggested, his gaze remaining shrewd. When The Major didn't appear the least bit interested in taking a chill pill, the chief said, "I can appreciate your concern for your daughter given recent events, but Agent Fallon is a highly skilled investigator with combat training. She's more than capable of taking care of herself."

"My daughter was almost killed last night," The Major said in a hard tone. "This investigation is stirring up hornets' nests that don't need stirring."

Jane blinked. "Dad...do you know something? Do you know who's behind all this?"

The Major cast her a short glance with a curt, "No" before returning to the chief. "But I do know that whoever is pulling the strings is not going to stop until whoever is poking at things is compelled to quit. Last night was a warning."

She suppressed a shudder. "All the more reason why we can't stop now," she said, ignoring her dad's building rage at being denied obedience. "Listen, I thought we'd found all the answers to this case when I originally closed it. I was wrong, and I aim to close it properly this time. I will find whoever is behind this corruption and I will carve it out with a dull spoon if I have to."

"Someone is going to carve *you* up if you're not careful," her dad countered.

She took a page from Holden's playbook. "They'd have to catch me first. They caught me off guard is all. It happened once. It won't happen again. Besides, we have some new leads and we're closing in—I can feel it." Okay, so maybe that was a bit of an embellishment, but she sure as hell wasn't going to admit to her father they'd fallen flat on their faces with their last lead and they were going on fumes. Nope. She'd rather eat a toenail than admit that to him. She had to bring home a win, otherwise her father would never see her as anything more than a weak female who always needed protection and couldn't handle herself in a fight. She squared her shoulders and looked to the chief. "The attempt on my life only cements our theory that we are on to something. Someone is getting nervous."

"I have to agree," the chief said, then addressed The Major. "Agents Fallon and Archangelo are my two best investigators. If anyone can figure this out, it's them. Let's give them a chance."

The Major drew himself up. "Chief Harris, it seems to me this case is more suited to the FBI than the CIA. You're muddying jurisdictional lines, don't you think?"

"Not at all. Miko Archangelo's case landed in our jurisdiction due to the potential international threat to our country, as well as the military connection. This was, and still remains, a CIA case. We are well within our rights to hold on to this case."

Displeased, The Major pinned the chief with a wintry glare. "Do you have children, Chief Harris?"

"Yes. A daughter."

The Major made a faintly aggrieved face. "Then you understand the limitations of the weaker sex. It's not their fault—blame genetics. Jane is a fine agent, suitable for desk tasks, but for dangerous missions I would prefer you consider what you would do if it were your daughter facing certain death and then act accordingly."

Rage and despair at being humiliated in front her boss made something toxic burn at the back of Jane's throat, and she fought to keep it down. How could he embarrass her like that? To openly call her weak in front of her superior? Heat seared her cheeks as she tried to keep her composure. "Your input is neither appreciated nor warranted," she told her father, then she looked to the chief. "Excuse me, Chief Harris, but Holden and I have a new lead to chase down. Dad, I'm sure you can see yourself out."

Jane didn't wait for his reaction because she didn't care what else he had to say on the matter. She bolted from the office, jerked her jacket from her desk, scooped up her cooling coffee and barked to Holden, "Let's go."

Holden, a smart man, quickly followed.

Once they were inside the car, she allowed everything to fall out in a stream of angry, hurt and dizzying barrage of words. "How dare he do that to me! I've spent my entire life feeling as if I need to apologize for being the wrong gender and I've always had to go out of my way to be more than just a weak female, but it doesn't matter what I do. That's all he'll ever see me as! Would he do that to Walker or Ian? Hell no. Of course not, because they're men and they can take care of themselves. Of all the self-righteous, misguided, sexist bullshit my father has ever spouted from his mouth—this takes the ever-lovin' cake!"

"I'm going to take a guess things didn't go well in there?" Holden rested his arm on the steering wheel as he regarded her with faint concern. "Mind if you clue me in so I can be righteously indignant with you?"

She cast him an impatient look. "I'm not in the mood for jokes."

"I'm not joking," he insisted, saying, "I'm completely serious. If he's made you this upset, clearly he's an idiot."

"Don't call my dad an idiot," she whipped back with a warning. "He's still my dad and I love him, even if he is a jerk."

"Oh, sorry. I'm new to the rules of this particular game," he said with a small grin.

She sighed, bouncing her head softly on the headrest. "Why is he so...*The Major* at all times? Why can't he just be my *dad*? And a *normal* dad at that? You know, he's never given me a true compliment that wasn't prefaced or followed by some kind of dig because I'm a woman? Every accomplishment comes with a caveat. It's as if he can't possibly acknowledge my skills with honest appreciation because that might challenge his long-held beliefs that women are inferior." She closed her eyes and groaned. "Why couldn't I have been born a man?"

"That would make our relationship awkward," Holden said, and she giggled in spite of her anger. She opened her eyes and stared at Holden, wondering why she felt safe sharing such personal information with him. She needed to vent and she knew he would keep her confidence.

He drew a deep breath and said, "Listen, I'm not the most experienced advice giver when it comes to dealing with difficult dads. Me and Miko split from our dad as soon as possible and we never looked back. To be fair, I don't think our dad cared one way or the other. By the time we were seventeen, we were just two rivals living in his house and eating his food. Once he even accused Miko of coming on to his skank girlfriend. Like that would happen. If anything, she came on to Miko and it just about scarred him for life. It's probably the reason he wanted to join the military, because after that woman dropped her towel in front of him, Miko figured there was nothing left out there to shock him."

"She dropped her towel in front of him?"

"Yeah. Horrifying. Did I mention she was a meth addict? No meat on her bones, pocked skin and terrible teeth. Honestly, it could've turned a man against women in general if she'd tried to do more than just entice him with her less-than-stellar goods."

She shouldn't laugh, but damn, Holden had a way of tickling her funny bone when she least expected it. "You're something else, Archangelo," she said, appreciating him just a smidge more, even if her feelings for him were becoming more confused by the minute. "Thanks."

"Hey, that's what I'm here for. Well, that and giving mind-blowing orgasms, of course. That's the very definition of partner with benefits. Didn't you know that?"

She groaned. "I hate that term."

"Really? Okay, let's brainstorm, then. Personally, I like *secret lovah* because it sounds so taboo, but in a classy way, or how about *booty-call benefactor,* but honestly that seems like a mouthful—and not in a good way. Or there's always—"

"Good God, please stop," she begged, shaking her head. "There aren't even words. Can we just put this conversation on the back burner for now and focus on the case? I'd rather put my brain to work doing something productive, okay?"

"You got it." He turned the key in the ignition. Before he put the car in Drive, he put his hand over Jane's. "Listen, I don't care what your dad says—I wouldn't want anyone else on this case with me. I trust you, Fallon. And I'm not just saying that because of our...unique relationship. Okay?"

Tears welled anew in her eyes and she wondered how she'd never seen Holden's true integrity shining past the facade he wore every day. "Thank you," she said with stark gratitude. "I needed to hear that."

"I know you did." He put the car in Drive. "Time to work."

"Amen," she murmured, more than ready to put

her mind to work, although as they drove to the bank where Miko had his safety deposit box, she wondered how the hell her father had known so quickly that she'd been shot at. A disquieting thought raced through her mind. What if her father had known because he'd arranged it? The Major was known for getting things done. Maybe he thought if he scared her, she'd startle like a little bunny and scamper off for the shelter of the underbrush, cowering like a female is wont to do—in her father's eyes.

That's a pretty far-fetched theory, Fallon. Yeah… probably. Her gaze followed the street-side scenery as her mind zinged in all kinds of crazy directions. What the hell? How could she even think that? Obviously, she was sleep deprived because her father was a lot of things, but he wasn't a cold-blooded killer and he certainly wouldn't hurt his own daughter. But even if he didn't call for the hit, the fact that her father knew was enough to make her gut ache. "I want to know how my dad knew about the hit," she said out loud. Maybe Holden would have some additional insight.

He frowned. "Your guess is as good as mine." He seemed perplexed. "All I can say is that his connections are pretty deep. Maybe someone heard it over dispatch and recognized the address? I don't know." He paused a moment to peer at her. "You don't think…"

"No," she said quickly. Just the shameful thought was enough to make her want to cover her head and hide. "My father would never do anything so despicable."

"I have to agree with you. I just wanted to make sure you weren't worried about it. That kind of thing could mess with your head."

"Tell me about it," she grumbled. "This whole situation has me staring at shadows looking for clues."

"It's enough to make you go cross-eyed. I wonder if that's how Miko felt. He never knew who he could trust, and the people he could trust, he didn't want to get involved. He must've felt very isolated."

She nodded and tenderly rubbed his cheek with her knuckles. "Thank you for talking me down and listening to me rant. I don't usually lose control like that."

"Maybe you need to."

She cast him a speculative glance before chuckling. "Yeah. Maybe I do. Felt good."

"So what'd you say to your dad while you were in there?" he asked.

"I basically told him to stop treating me like a child. He completely embarrassed me in front of the chief. It's one thing to be treated a certain way around family, but not out in the real world where you're respected in your field. It would be the equivalent of me dressing down my father in front of his old military cronies. It would humiliate him, which is why I would never do that. However, when it comes to me, he doesn't think twice about throwing me under the bus, and I don't understand what I've ever done to deserve being treated like that."

"You haven't done anything. That's the point of being a sexist jerk. Sorry, but it's the facts. He doesn't see you as a capable person in your own right—just as a woman who either needs protecting or subjugating."

"God, you're right," she moaned, hating that her father was so wrong about everything having to do with the female gender.

"Kinda makes you wonder if he treated your mom that way. If so, I'd leave his ass, too. Sorry, I know that's a touchy subject."

She glared even though what he said made sense. She'd never suffer a man to treat her like that in a relationship, though why she allowed her father to do so was a perplexing psychological puzzle. "Well, maybe she left because of him, or maybe she left because she was weak…who knows? It doesn't change the fact he embarrassed the ever-loving hell out of me back there and I said a few things that, if I don't end up backing up with proof, are going to bite me in the ass."

"Such as?" Holden asked, worried.

Jane sighed. "Let's just hope this safety deposit box provides some answers. Another dead end would only prove my father right."

Holden nodded in understanding. So much was riding on this case. More so than some political intrigue. She needed to prove something to her father and Holden needed to clear his brother's name. This case was about family. Screw the intrigue. Plain and simple…this case was about family.

Chapter 19

Holden and Jane arrived at First National Bank and Trust and walked straight to the bank manager, flashing their credentials and causing the pencil-thin man to eye them warily. "Good morning, agents. What can I do for you today?"

"We're here to open a safety deposit box belonging to my brother, Miko Archangelo," Holden answered. After reading the man's badge, he added, "Any help you could give us, Mr. Olgivey, would be most appreciated."

"Do you have the key?"

Holden pulled the key from his pocket and handed it to the manager. "And where is Mr. Archangelo, if I may ask?"

"He's dead."

Mr. Olgivey nodded and gestured for them to follow. Holden and Jane exchanged looks. Well, that went smoothly. Perhaps a little too smoothly? They passed through the security gates to the private receiving room and waited as the bank manager opened the box and placed it on the small table. "Your brother was an interesting man. He told me that someday his brother might come for his box. I suppose that day is here," he said, surprising Holden. "If there's anything else you require, I'll be waiting outside." Then the man let himself out and closed the door behind him.

"That was strange," Jane observed. "What do you think that was about?"

"Who knows? I'll worry about the bank manager later. Right now I want to know what's inside this thing."

Holden opened the metal box and removed several papers, stacks of more cash and a thumb drive. He stared at the scant items and frowned. "That's it?" he exclaimed, disappointed and frustrated. "What the hell kind of cat-and-mouse game was my brother playing?"

Jane gathered up the paperwork and began sorting through it. "Property deeds. Seems your brother owned some undeveloped land in California...."

He sighed. "Yeah, he talked about building a hunting cabin up in the mountains like Nathan's. I guess he finally got around to purchasing the land but never got the chance to put the rest of his plan into action. Damn it," he said under his breath, fighting the urge to punch the wall or break a chair. His gaze fell on the thumb drive at the same time Jane's did. He met her questioning stare and shrugged. "Your guess is as good as mine. We'll need a computer to open it."

"What about all this cash?" Jane asked, pushing the stacks around and counting. "At least another twenty thousand is here. It seems your brother was stockpiling cash for some reason. Paranoid much?"

He cast a dark look her way. "Not so paranoid if our suspicions are correct."

Immediately contrite, she said, "I'm sorry, Holden. I didn't mean to be insensitive."

He waved away her apology, irritated at himself for being a touchy puss. "No worries. I'm just frustrated. Sorry for snapping at you."

"It's okay." Her gaze strayed to the cash, and he knew what she was thinking, so he decided to just meet it head-on.

"I'll run the cash through the system to make sure it's not stolen," he assured her. She visibly relaxed. "But my brother wasn't a thief. I can guarantee you that."

"Are you his sole heir?"

"Yeah."

"Seems if it comes back clean, you've come into a fair bit of cash if you count the money still locked away in those foreign accounts."

He shrugged. Money didn't mean any more to him than it'd meant to Miko. He tucked the thumb drive into his pocket and returned the deed and the money to the box. "I'd rather have my brother back." And that was the damn truth. Money didn't mean anything if it came at such a high cost. "Let's go."

Holden was slipping into a black mood, and he couldn't seem to stop himself. He was tired of dead ends and cryptic clues that sent him running in the opposite direction. Was this what it had been like for Miko, trying to stay one step ahead of whoever was after him? Things would've been different if Miko had trusted him enough to just level with him. Maybe he'd still be alive. Or maybe they'd both be dead. Who knew?

Jane touched his arm. "I have a feeling there's something on this thumb drive that's going to be worth our while. Nobody keeps junk in their safety deposit box."

"Maybe."

"No maybe about it," she disagreed firmly, not letting him lose hope. "Listen, I know we've hit a brick wall a time or two, but we must be getting close if people are starting to shoot at us, right?"

A small smile found him. "Yeah, I guess so."

"Okay, then. No more pity parties. We got this. Let's head back to the office, fire up this thumb drive and see what was so important that Miko had to hide it in a bank box."

Holden nodded, thankful for Jane's cool head when he got stuck in his own loop of despair. She was a good partner. Hell, she was a good person. "You know, I really underestimated you before," he admitted. "I mean, I didn't try to see beyond the surface, and I'm sorry. I wish I had sooner. I couldn't have done this without you." She blushed prettily and he was gripped by the urge to plant a kiss on her pouty, sensual-without-even-trying lips. He held back. Now was not the time. But later, he promised himself. "How about dinner tonight? Let me take you out to a nice restaurant. Like a date."

Her smile faded. She tucked a chunk of hair behind her ear, her gaze clearing with no-nonsense seriousness, and he knew whatever ground he'd gained he'd just lost. "I'm not sure we should. Already things have gotten muddied, and please don't take this the wrong way because you've been there for me when I needed someone, but everything in our lives is such a mess that I don't think we need to add to it, okay?"

"Jane, when are you going to admit you want to be with me? It'd save us both a lot of energy if you'd stop fighting what you feel."

Her blush deepened and she scowled. "Can we focus on the case, please? I don't want to get into it right now. My dad is going to want to talk to me after I blew up at him in the chief's office and I don't want to have to explain you, too."

Ah…so he was going to remain her dirty little secret. Ordinarily, that wouldn't bother him because he rarely stuck around long enough to care. But with Jane, he cared.

He cared a lot.

They continued the rest of the drive in silence. Back at the office, they immediately headed to Holden's computer to open the thumb drive. Encrypted password protection stonewalled them. "You've got to be kidding me," he muttered, sliding his hand through his hair and wanting to scream. "C'mon, Miko. Cut me some slack, will ya?"

"We can give it to IT," Jane said. "They can probably jail break it."

"I don't trust anyone with this thumb drive. For all I know, my brother died protecting whatever is on it." He leaned back in his chair, thinking hard. All lines pointed in one direction. He swore under his breath and knew he didn't have a choice. "James Cotton."

Jane nodded and lifted her shoulder. "Well, at least you've got some more disposable cash to offer the little tech mercenary."

"True enough."

"All right, so we'll table that for later tonight. In the meantime, we'll visit Dr. Odgers at the Department of Defense. We need to talk with her anyway."

He nodded, knowing Jane was right. Besides, what could he do but wait and see what James's asking price would be for cracking into the thumb drive? Not much. Better to be active than sit on his ass doing nothing. He tucked the drive in his pocket and gestured as he swung his jacket back onto his shoulders. "Saddle up. Let's go talk to Kat."

Jane had heard a few things about Dr. Odgers, but she'd never actually met the supposedly brilliant scientist. Honestly, Jane found the idea of meeting with a genius intimidating, even though she wasn't dumb by any means.

When they arrived, they were cleared by security and then escorted through several more levels of clearance before they reached the state-of-the-art lab where Dr. Odgers worked.

Impeccably clean glass doors opened with a whisper at their arrival, and they passed through to find a willowy woman with her hair tucked into a messy bun wearing a lab coat and talking to an assistant. "Dr. Odgers?" Jane ventured, and the woman startled, pushing her glasses farther up the bridge of her nose. She smiled uncertainly until she saw Holden. "Oh! I heard you were coming. I'm so glad to see you!" She went straight to him and shook his hand vigorously. "You know, I never really got the chance to properly thank you for all your help in rescuing Jake during that whole abysmal situation with MCX-209. Horrid. Absolutely horrid. I still have nightmares about it all."

"He's a good man. I was happy to be a part of that mission," Holden said with the solemn integrity that was as part of him as breath. Jane waited to be properly introduced, and Holden did so a heartbeat later. "Dr. Odgers—"

"Please call me Kat. Dr. Odgers is way too formal for what we went through together. Facing certain death has a way of making you realize that all that silly formality is just for show."

He acquiesced with a slight tip of his head and began again. "Kat, I would like you to meet CIA agent Jane Fallon."

"A pleasure," Kat said, pushing her glasses again and shaking Jane's hand just as vigorously as she had Holden's. "What's the occasion? Want a tour of the lab? It's mind-blowing what the government has in resources. I would've died and gone to heaven at Tessara if I'd had access to such state-of-the-art equipment."

"Wasn't Tessara well funded?"

"Oh, yes, but I was a lower-level scientist so it's not as if I got the corner office, if you know what I mean."

"I guess that all changed the minute you created the Game Changer," Jane said, and Kat's expression darkened into a scowl.

"Please don't call it that. MCX-209 was an embarrassing failure and only that psychopath, Miles Jogan, and his bimbo, Camille, called it that."

Miles and Camille, formerly of the Defense Intelligence Agency, currently serving time for a host of crimes against the nation—and human beings in general—had been the ringleaders behind the plot to weaponize and consequently sell MCX-209 to the highest bidder. But in the process, they'd made Kat test the drug on human subjects, most of whom had died, with the exception of Kat's husband, Jake.

"Not exactly," Jane corrected, taking Kat aback. "Did you know Penny Winslow was monitoring your progress on that particular drug way before you started administering your drug trials?"

"What are you talking about?"

Holden held up his hand and said, "Is there someplace we can talk in private? This is a sensitive topic and we're not sure who all is listening, if you catch my drift."

"Oh, great. More secret government spy stuff,"

Kat grumbled. She motioned for them to follow her into her office. Once they were safely closed inside, she dropped into a leather-backed chair and said, "All right, now start again. Penny Winslow was watching my experiments?"

"Yes. It appears she also dubbed MCX-209 the Game Changer, possibly before Miles Jogan did. In fact, it might've been Penny who christened the drug in the first place. Did you ever have any contact with her?"

Kat shook her head. "No. All my contact was with my supervisor—"

"Hector Olonzo," Jane supplied. As Kat nodded, Jane added, "He's dead."

Kat's stare widened and she gasped in shock. "What happened? Hector was so sweet. On Tuesdays he always brought me caramel cookies from the snack cart."

"He was killed in a mugging gone wrong, but I'll be honest, I don't think it was an accident," Holden admitted.

"What do you mean?"

Jane held the woman's gaze. "He means we think someone may have killed Hector to keep him quiet. He was a loose end that someone needed to snip."

Kat's hand flew to her throat as she realized what they were saying. "Do you mean…I'm a loose end, too?"

"Potentially," Holden said. "But not yet. You're the only one with knowledge of how MCX-209 works. But, honestly, we don't even know if that's what this is all about. My brother killed himself and left behind a lot of unanswered questions that all seem to circle back to Tessara in one form or another."

"I understand," Kat murmured with a nod. "But MCX-209 has been shut down. The whole reason I agreed to come to work here was so I could be assured that no one else would get their hands on the formula."

"So you would know if anyone was poking around?"

Kat nodded. "Heck yes. I'm the lead scientist here. I answer directly to Director Michelle Rainier, and she answers to the president. I made sure of it. I don't want anyone ever getting their hands on that horrid drug."

"How is Jake holding up?" Holden asked quietly.

At the mention of her husband and the one person still recovering from an injection of the drug, Kat brightened. "Oh, he's doing so well! I'd say almost recovered and still going strong. He has minor gaps in his memory, but it seems to correlate with his interest in whatever he's doing, such as not doing the dishes when I ask him."

Jane and Holden chuckled. "Glad to hear he's on the mend," Holden said. "He's a good man."

Kat grinned, eyes sparkling behind her glasses. "I think so, too."

Jane cleared her throat and brought the topic back into focus. "It seems Penny Winslow was actively involved in a few other projects—Switchblade, Carousel, Serenade. Any of those ring a bell?"

Kat pursed her lips as she searched her memory but ultimately shook her head. "No, I was pretty focused on my own project. I truly thought I was on to something big."

"It was big, all right—just not what you thought it was going to be for," Holden said. "Do you keep samples of MCX-209 here on the premises?"

"Yes, why?"

"Would you mind checking to see that everything is where it should be?" Holden asked. "MCX-209 and Tessara seem to be the only common denominators, and we're grasping at straws."

"Sure. I can't take you into the restricted area, but I can show you the live feed from the security line."

"You have a video camera trained on the samples?" Jane asked incredulously. "That must make for some really boring footage."

"Very. But it's a clean room and only certain people have enough clearance to even access that portion of the building." She logged onto her computer and quickly brought up the live feed. Several tubes of blue liquid were suspended in liquid nitrogen, frozen for safekeeping. "See? All good and accounted for. The feed is also time-stamped for additional security. If there's a single, tiny blip in the time feed, it'll alert security. And so far, it's been quiet."

Jane released a pent-up breath. "That's good to know. That drug—and the fact that it's real—freaks me out."

"Yeah, it's pretty scary in action, too," Kat said with a bleak expression. "Anyway, you don't have to worry about this particular baddie getting out there in the world."

Holden nodded. "I guess we've taken up enough of your time. Listen, watch your back. Until we figure out who's all behind this, don't trust anyone."

Kat smiled nervously. "Boy, and here I thought I was done with dodging people trying to kill me."

Holden crooked a charming grin and said, "For me, that's a typical Thursday."

Jane rolled her eyes and gave him a slight push toward the door. "Okay, Mr. Bond, let's go. We have to find a way to break into this thumb drive."

"Oh, I can do that for you," Kat offered with an unexpected smile, adding shyly, "I'm a bit of a technogeek in my spare time. I could've been a hacker in a different life."

Jane liked this odd scientist woman. For all her admitted geekiness, she had a warmth to her. Holden produced the thumb drive and handed it to Kat. "Good luck. Work your magic. It seems to be encrypted—"

"No offense, but I break encryptions when I can't sleep at night. Well, it's either that or memorize formulas. Depends on my mood," Kat said brightly, accepting the drive and pushing it into the USB port on her computer. "Let's see how ambitious this encryption is."

Jane glanced at Holden and saw his anxious expression. They needed a bit of hope today. Within a few minutes, Kat chortled with a happy squee of excitement like a little kid, her feet dancing on the floor as she motioned with a "Ta-da!" for them both to join her behind the desk. "No problem-o. This was easy-peasy. Whoever encrypted it wasn't really serious about keeping people out. Now, who does this belong to?"

"My brother, Miko. He kept it in a safety deposit box along with some cash," Holden answered, peering over Kat's shoulder. He looked to Kat and said, "Mind if I poke around?"

"Be my guest." She rolled out of the way to give Holden more room. "Do you know what you're looking for?"

"Not a clue." But Holden and Jane saw soon enough what was on that drive, and it took Jane's breath away. Holden doubled-clicked the file marked Insurance Policy, and suddenly everything came into focus. "Am I looking at what I think I'm looking at?"

"It looks like a hit list," Jane answered under her breath, shocked. "I recognize some of these names from restricted files. These are I.D. hits."

"That's a lot of names," Kat observed with a worried expression. "Why would he keep this?"

"He called it his insurance policy for a reason. Someone doesn't want this information going public. I suppose Penny Winslow would've been pretty threatened by the knowledge that this list exists."

Jane nodded, pointing. "Click on the file marked Key."

Holden double-clicked and another set of notes opened on the screen. "You're kidding me." He shook his head. "This isn't good."

Jane looked to Kat. "Are you sure no one's been working on MCX-209 without your permission?"

"I'm positive," Kat answered. "Why?"

"Because according to Miko's notes, someone authorized another trial of the drug."

"That's impossible." Kat shook her head. "I supervise all experiments in this lab. Nothing gets by without my knowledge."

Holden frowned. "Someone's planning something with that drug. Maybe Miko was on to whoever had put plans into motion."

"If so, why didn't he just tell you?" Jane asked, sagging at the enormity of the situation. "Maybe we could've helped."

"I ask myself that question a hundred times a day and I still don't have a suitable answer," Holden said, scrolling through the notes, searching for clues. "Every single day."

Kat, visibly shaken by the realization that her drug was still sought after by the wrong people, said, "Listen, I hate to cut this short, but I have to talk to my boss about this. If someone is circumventing our security, we have to find out how and why."

"Can you trust your boss?"

Kat nodded emphatically. "Yes. She's the one who helped take down Miles and Camille, and she shut down The Compound. She's going to want to know about this newest development."

"If you feel confident without a shadow of a doubt that you can trust her…" Jane let it trail. If it were her, she wouldn't trust anyone outside of this room, especially given the history of that drug. It was the scientist's call, though.

"I do," Kat said, looking devastated. "I can't believe this is happening again. I wish I'd never created that stupid drug."

"Well, think of it this way—you never would've met Jake if you hadn't," Holden said, trying to cheer her up even though the situation was pretty dire for everyone involved.

Jane suppressed the immediate flood of warmth at his show of kindness toward the scientist. He was such a good guy. Why couldn't she just forget about her family and let her heart decide?

"Hey, have you ever heard of a winery called Butterfly Bend?" Holden asked Kat, switching gears quickly.

"Um…yeah, I think that's the winery owned by Penny Winslow's cousin. He came by Tessara a few times. They were real close, I guess. Why?"

"I don't know. Miko mentioned Butterfly Bend in his notes and we visited the winery and talked with the owner. He seems like a nice guy. He said Tessara was working on creating a cork that didn't disintegrate with time and protected the integrity of the wine. Sound familiar?"

"Not really. Then again, I was hyperfocused on my own trials. I don't doubt that Tessara was doing exactly that for him as a favor to Penny. Like I said, he and Penny seemed really close. Almost like brother and sister."

Jane pocketed that information. From the expression on Holden's face, he seemed to find that nugget interesting, too, even if they didn't know how the pieces fit together. He pulled the thumb drive free from the USB port and tucked it back in his pocket. "Thanks for all your help, Kat," he said, moving away from the computer and heading for the door. "Remember what I said—don't trust anyone if you can help it. Keep your circle of trust tight, and just to be on the safe side, go ahead and clue Jake in on this newest development. Wouldn't hurt to have him keeping an eye on things."

"He's going to freak out when I tell him." Kat grimaced. "But I'm a terrible liar, so he'll find out sooner or later anyway."

Holden smiled and thanked Kat once more, then they were escorted from the building.

"Is it just me or does this plot get more and more convoluted by the second?" Jane asked, glancing at Holden wearily. "I can't make heads or tails of which direction we're supposed to be traveling anymore. Tessara, MCX-209, fake IDs, hit lists…where does it end?"

"It ends with us finding out what really happened to my brother and who tried to shoot you," Holden answered grimly, pulling everything back into focus. "All the pieces are there. We just need to put the puzzle together."

"If you say so." Jane felt a headache coming on. "I think I need a beer."

"Now you're talking my language." He grinned, and her heart did a funny flip-flop that was entirely too telling for her liking, but what could she do? It seemed useless to fight what was happening between them. She knew without a doubt she could put on a show of keeping him at a distance, though by the end of the night, there was nowhere she'd rather be than snuggled up tight against his side. What a lovely mess they'd created.

"Fine, but I'm buying," she said almost grumpily, and he laughed.

"Far be it from me to turn down such a charming offer. Now tell me you're going to throw me down and have your wicked way with me, too, and I'll be a happy man," he said with a wink. She groaned. *Lord help us both.*

She climbed into the car and barked, "Get in the car before I make you walk."

"I love a take-charge woman," he laughed, climbing in beside her. "Especially when you do that thing with your—"

"If you value your life, stop," she warned, fighting the blush in her cheeks. His laughter tickled her insides, but she refused to give in. She may know the score between them, but damn it, she didn't have to be happy about it.

Chapter 20

Kat Odgers hurried to her boss's office, her soft lab shoes making light squeaking noises as she went. She found Michelle on the phone, but immediately went in anyway, shut the door behind her and waited somewhat patiently for her boss to finish her conversation.

Michelle, noting Kat's agitation, ended the call and looked to Kat with a raised brow. "Everything okay?"

"No. Everything is not okay. In fact, everything is pretty messed up and I don't know what to think."

"Okay, calm down. Start at the beginning. What's wrong?"

"Someone is poking around MCX-209 and restarting the trials." At that, Michelle paused and leaned back in her chair. Kat immediately felt panicked. "What a minute…you already knew this? How is that possible? You promised me that I would be in charge of MCX-209."

"Have a seat, Kat," Michelle suggested, but Kat didn't want to sit. She wanted answers. Her hands began to shake. When Kat continued to stand, Michelle said, "You are in charge of the initial formula, but there have been some preliminary trials of the modified version of MCX-209 that you formulated to save Jake."

"What?" Kat nearly screeched, her heart thundering in her chest. "What are you saying? Someone is testing that formula without my involvement? You promised me that wouldn't happen!"

"And I firmly stood behind that promise, but some things are above my pay grade."

Kat blinked. "How is that possible? You answer to the president."

"Yes, I do, and it's my job to ensure that we are in control of one of the most dangerous drugs on the planet, and we can't be in control if we don't understand how it works."

"It works by erasing memory," Kat said, wiping at the tears gathering in her eyes. "My husband suffered the most unimaginable horror of losing who he was. You know that! And what about the people who died when Miles forced me to inject them with the first test formula? Their brains leaked from their ears! I'll never forget their faces and how they trusted me not to hurt them."

"That wasn't your fault," Michelle reminded her, but Kat didn't want her platitudes. "Kat, I need you to calm down and listen to me. I should've told you, but I didn't want to upset you, which, judging by your reaction, was a wise decision."

"It wasn't wise. It was deceptive," Kat said hotly. "This drug should've been destroyed completely. It has no acceptable application, and the fact you lied to me means you're no better than Miles Jogan, tricking me into working for the very people who were responsible for this horror in my life."

"You're overreacting," Michelle said, losing patience, but Kat didn't care. She felt betrayed and, worse, terrified that the nightmare was about to start all over again. "The clinical trials are limited and supervised. You have nothing to fear."

"You're wrong," Kat said flatly, wiping at her tears. "This is going to end badly. That drug is evil and it brings terrible things wherever it goes."

"Kat…please. You're a scientist. Let's be sensible. Now that you're aware of the situation, we'd like to include you in the trials. It goes without saying your expertise in this is invaluable."

"I need to think," Kat said, moving to the door. "I thought I could trust you—"

"You can," Michelle insisted with a subtle frown, as if distressed by the realization that Kat felt betrayed. "Listen, I understand your concerns. I'd be lying if I said I didn't share them, but this was taken out of my hands."

"What do you mean?" she asked. "No one is higher than the president."

"I can't elaborate more than I have. Trust me when I say MCX-209 will not fall into the wrong hands."

"Sorry, but obviously, it already has." Kat held up her hand, halting Michelle; she'd heard enough. "I...I have to talk to Jake. This is...horrible, horrible news."

Before Michelle could say anything else, Kat bolted. She needed air. She needed clarity. Most of all, she needed Jake. Jake would know what to do.

Michelle watched Kat leave her office and exhaled a troubled sigh. Truthfully, the drug and its potential ramifications scared the hell out of her—and well it should—but as she'd told Kat, the directive came to her from very high channels. She tapped her fingers lightly on her desk, worried by Kat's reaction. What had she expected? Kat had suffered grievously at the hands of the drug and she certainly wouldn't welcome the idea that someone was tinkering with the formula. As much as she didn't want to, Michelle had to make a phone call.

She dialed the number, heart in her throat. "Dr. Odgers has found out the formula is back in active research," she said, swallowing the lump in her throat. "And she's very unhappy."

"That's unfortunate. Can you persuade her to get on board?"

"Not likely. She has every reason to hate MCX-209 and its potential ramifications."

"You like her."

Michelle didn't bother lying. "I do. She's a brilliant scientist and a good person."

"The world has plenty of brilliant scientists. If you value this one in particular, find a way to persuade her to get on board. Otherwise, she's a liability." A beat followed before the person on the other end said, "And how exactly did Dr. Odgers find out about this newest development?"

"Two CIA agents are investigating Miko Archangelo's death. Somehow they connected the dots."

"Yes, I'm well aware of those two. They've been poking around Tessara. Up until now I didn't think they had anything of interest. Seems I was wrong."

"I did as you asked," Michelle said, curling her fingers around the phone. "I held up my end of the bargain."

"Yes, we are pleased with your cooperation. We will be in touch."

"My sister..."

"She's fine for now, but I suspect her health may decline if you aren't able to persuade Dr. Odgers to be more helpful."

Sweat gathered along Michelle's hairline. "How am I supposed to do that?"

"That's your problem. You're a smart woman. You'll figure something out."

The line went dead, and Michelle replaced the phone with cold, shaking fingers. She was living in a nightmare. How had this happened? Tessara was the epicenter for all evil. She swallowed and willed herself to stop shaking, to think. Her gaze swept her office, knowing that somewhere a bug was nestled, catching her every word, her every movement. Contact had been made four months ago, soon after she'd busted Miles Jogan and Camille Stephens, shutting down their horror show featuring MCX-209. If only Michelle had known that she'd merely poked the dragon. Miles and Camille hadn't been the ringleaders. No, whoever was really pulling the strings was far more powerful than she'd imagined. And worse, she had no clue who was in charge.

And they had her younger sister as leverage. Michelle, as tough as they came, former marine, was held hostage by fear, weakened by her love for her sister.

Hang tight, Hilary. Just stay alive.

A plan—reckless and razor's-edge dangerous—took root.

Kat couldn't stop pacing. It was something she did out of nervous habit because it helped her think, but tonight her brain was just too filled with chaotic ramblings and frightened gibberish to be calmed by any amount of pacing. "They're going to do something terrible with that drug—I can feel it," she told Jake, nearly hysterical. "And you should've seen Michelle…cold as ice. I've never seen her so distant and mean. I thought we were friends! But she's using me, just like Miles and Camille did. But this is far worse than what they did because I didn't like them. I liked Michelle. I believed in her. I believed in what I was doing for the greater good. What a sap

I still am, still trying to see the good in people when I know for a fact—having seen the worst—that people can be totally evil."

"Calm down," Jake said gently. "Let's think this through."

"Calm down? Haven't you heard a thing I've said? MCX-209 is back in active research. That means somewhere in that government facility, someone is putting their hands all over my research in the hopes of finding the magic concoction for that wretched drug."

"Did she say how long the research has been going on?"

Kat shook her head. "No. I didn't ask. But what does this mean? She promised me no one would go near that drug or the research without my permission or authorization, and that was a flat-out lie. She lied to you, too!"

"Something doesn't feel right," Jake said, furrowing his brow in thought, remaining chill even as Kat was freaking out. Of course, that was one of the many reasons she loved him, but, c'mon, certainly she shouldn't be the only one jumping up and down in a total meltdown, right? Jake met her gaze and she stopped pacing for a moment. "Michelle isn't the kind of woman who goes back on her word. I've known her for many years. Something else is going on behind the scenes."

"Like what?"

"I don't know," he admitted. "But I'll bet it has

something to do with Holden and Jane poking around."

Kat nodded. "That's feasible, though I couldn't for the life of me tell you how. I mean, they were asking a lot of questions at Tessara, and they found out my old supervisor, Hector, is dead. One thing I've learned since hanging out with you and your friends—there's no such thing as a coincidence, right?"

"Exactly," Jake agreed, adding, "which is why I asked Holden and Jane to come over tonight."

Kat blinked. "You did?"

"Yes. I have some questions of my own to ask them, and now that the situation seems to be becoming more and more unstable, it's better to control the environment we're in. We have to assume your lab has been compromised, possibly bugged." Kat gasped and he continued with a nod, "Yeah, more than likely. It's what I would've done if the situation were reversed and I needed information. At least here in our home, we know we can speak freely."

"Why's that?"

He crooked a short grin that made her remember why she'd fallen for him in the first place. "Because I have antibug devices planted all over our home. Instant interference. Haven't you ever wondered why our cells don't work in the house?"

"D'oh!" she gasped softly as the knowledge sank in. "I just figured we were in a bad reception spot." She giggled briefly before sobering. "Okay, so what do you hope to find out from Holden and Jane?"

"Not sure, but if we put our heads together we

might be able to pinpoint where the threat is originating."

Her eyes suddenly watered and her lower lip trembled. "I don't want to go on the run again," she said as she climbed into his lap. His arms curled around her and she took momentary comfort in the solid feel of his touch. "The last time this happened, I almost lost you. I don't want to face that again. I would never step foot in another lab again if it meant you and I could live a normal life."

He chuckled and pressed a kiss to her forehead. "What is normal? It's been so long I don't remember."

"Not funny," she grumbled, pinching him for making jokes about something so serious. "I mean it. I can't go through this again. It was awful the first time around. I certainly don't want a repeat performance."

"Neither do I. I've only just started remembering how to tie my own shoes."

She laughed through the sheen of tears, loving him all the more that he could still joke, but it stung that she'd been the cause of his suffering. "I love you, Jake Isaacs," Kat said, wiping her nose with the back of her hand. "Don't you dare get yourself killed or I'll never forgive you."

"I love you more, Kat Isaacs. And I am too attached to living to get myself killed. I promise."

A shudder traveled through her. "Don't make promises you can't keep."

"I don't."

His solemn answer, devoid of laughter this time, reached into her heart and squeezed hard. She knew he'd do anything to protect her—even throw himself in the line of danger if it meant saving her life.

And that was what scared her the most.

Chapter 21

Holden and Jane, both surprised to get the call from Jake, hustled over to his house and were ushered in immediately. Holden shook Jake's hand and smiled. "You look better than the last time I saw you. At least now you're not drooling," he teased.

"I wasn't drooling," Jake shot back with mock irritation but broke it with a grin. "You look good, too. How are you doing?"

"Could be better, for sure. Things aren't exactly copacetic, if you know what I mean."

"I do," Jake agreed with a serious nod.

Holden quickly introduced Jane, and then all three walked into the living room, where a nervous Kat waited, biting her nails and fidgeting. "Good to see you again, Kat."

She smiled slightly but remained quiet. Jake handled the talking once they were all seated. "All right, unfortunately I didn't invite you over for board games and pizza. We've got a serious situation brewing. I've been down this road before and it's not pretty."

"So I've heard," Jane said. "You're pretty lucky to be alive, from what Holden has said."

"I'm lucky my wife is brilliant. If it weren't for her, I would be dead. She's the one who perfected the formula. Otherwise, my life would've ended with my brains leaking from my ears."

"It's not perfected," Kat protested, breaking her nervous silence to bounce from her chair and start pacing. "That's just it. It's just as dangerous as it ever was. I should've flushed everything down the toilet when I had the chance, but I was seduced by the idea of running my own state-of-the-art lab. This is my penance for having too big of an ego. This is karma."

"Kat, stop," Jake said gently, pulling her to him and soothing her frantic movements with a soft touch. "This isn't your fault. You have a gift for science. Okay? Stop berating yourself for something out of your control. We're going to get this figured out."

"What's going on? Something tells me we're missing a piece of the puzzle," Holden said.

"A big piece," Kat answered grimly, glancing at Jake for strength. "After you left, I went to my boss, Michelle, to confront her about the security break. She already knew! In fact, she'd authorized the active research, saying higher channels had given the clearance to bypass my involvement. She said it was out of her hands, but the PTB would like me back on board."

"Higher channels? Higher than the president?" Jane asked, confused.

"I don't know," Kat answered, just as confused. "I've never known Michelle to act like this. She was just as adamant as I was that MCX-209 end up locked away forever, but now she's changed her tune. It gave me a terrible stomachache and I immediately had diarrhea. Sorry for the TMI. When I get nervous I overshare."

Jake smiled indulgently at his wife and Holden felt a pang of envy for how in tune Kat and Jake were with one another. He stole a glance at Jane, and when he saw her wistful expression, he knew a moment of happiness, which was absurd, but it was there just the same.

Jane broke the silence first. "Is there any chance Michelle is working with someone at Tessara? My first guess is Ulysses Rocha. He gives me a corrupt vibe."

Kat wrung her hands. "Before today I would've said absolutely not, but I don't know what to think now."

"First and foremost, we need to figure out what the connection is between Tessara and whoever wants the research reactivated on MCX-209. What would anyone have to gain by restarting the study?"

"At first blush, I'd say world domination," Kat answered. "I mean, this drug is dangerous for many reasons. And if someone in high places is pushing the research, that must mean they already have something in mind for its use."

"Which certainly can't be good," Jake interjected, and Holden nodded.

A knock at the door startled them all. Everyone except Kat pulled a weapon. Kat laughed nervously. "Wouldn't we all feel dumb if it was just a pizza guy? Delivering a pizza we haven't ordered?" she tacked on with an audible gulp. Jane and Holden flanked the doorway while Jake prepared to open the door. He peered through the peephole and then pulled away with a quizzical expression. "It's Michelle," he mouthed before slowly opening the door. "Michelle? It's pretty late…what are you doing here?"

"I know how this looks, but it's not safe for me to talk outside. Will you invite me in? And act natural. I have eyes on me."

Jake nodded and ushered her inside, but everyone held their weapons at the ready.

"What are you doing here?" Kat asked. "What's going on?"

Michelle, dressed in a trench coat, shivered, her gaze sharp. "You were right. Something is going on. I couldn't say anything at the office. In fact, I haven't been able to say anything for months, and honestly, I was trying to keep you out of it for as long as possible, but time has run out. Someone blackmailed me into granting authorization for the active research. They have my sister, Hilary, and they've threatened her life if I didn't cover their tracks while they worked on your preliminary formula for the Game Changer."

"I wish people would stop calling it that," Kat groused. "Who is threatening you?"

"I haven't been able to figure that out. I only have a number that I've been unable to trace. They have my office and house bugged and I've been unable to make a move without them knowing about it. Frankly, I don't even know if it was safe to come here, except I'm supposed to be talking you into joining the research team. Otherwise, Hilary would be dead right now. For all I know, she already is dead."

"They haven't given you proof of life?" Jake asked.

Michelle shook her head. "Not in weeks. I fear the worst."

"You should've told someone," Holden said.

"I know, but I was afraid. She's the only family I have left. She's my kid sister and barely out of college. I never imagined something like this would ever happen. I never saw myself in a position where I couldn't protect myself or the ones I love. They struck where it hurt, and they knew exactly what to do to get me to cooperate."

"Sounds like a move Penny would make. If I didn't already know the bitch was dead, I'd say this was her doing," Holden said

"So who's at the heart of all this, then?" Jane asked the question they were all wondering. "Someone higher up in the food chain, for sure."

"How high are we talking?" Holden asked. "This goes pretty far if they're able to get to Michelle's level of clearance."

"My thoughts exactly," Jake said. "What do we know so far?"

"Well, it seems Miko was trying to gather enough evidence to bring down someone big, but he was so paranoid he left only cryptic clues. We have a list of ID hits, some connection to Butterfly Bend winery, Tessara Pharm and a really rampant information leak at high levels." Holden rubbed his jaw. "Now we also have someone wanting research to resume on MCX-209 and using Michelle to get it done. All in all, we've got a whole lot of loose ends and no way to tie them together."

"Not necessarily," Jane disagreed slowly, and Holden could see her mind working. "We know Penny Winslow was tight with her cousin, the owner of Butterfly Bend, and that Butterfly Bend was chosen for the Presidential Reserve wine, and the wine is being shipped at the end of this month for an executive dinner. We also know Tessara helped create the chemical coating for the cork used by Butterfly Bend. What if—and this is a wild theory—someone is planning to use those wine corks to spike the Presidential Reserve with MCX-209? Butterfly Bend has already been vetted, so it would easily pass the sniff test, putting the most dangerous drug on the planet right at the president's table."

"Holy crap," Holden breathed, his gaze widening at the very idea. "That's brilliant."

"But why?" Kat asked.

"Because the best way to take out an enemy is a surprise attack," Jake answered, his mouth tightening to a firm line. "If this is true, we're all targets, because a plan of this magnitude would've taken lots of careful planning and zero tolerance for loose ends. And every single one of us in this room is a loose end."

"Not again," Kat wailed, flopping into a chair and gripping her stomach with a groan. "There goes my stomach. Oh! Excuse me..." She ran for the restroom, leaving the rest of the group wrestling with their own nerves.

"We're in deep trouble," Jane murmured, glancing at Holden. "No wonder no one wanted this investigation reopened. We're talking the highest level of treason if you're right."

"I know." Holden knew in his bones they'd stumbled on the right theory, the one that'd cost Miko his life. But how to prove it without losing their own heads? Where to start? How to begin? "Time to put our heads together. We need answers and we need them by first light or else we all better polish up our passports because life in the States will no longer be possible. They'll find us, and when they do, it'll be lights out."

"I'll start the coffee," Jake said. "It's going to be a long night."

Several hours into brainstorming leads, Jane stumbled across something they'd missed. "Do you remember when we went to Tessara, we were greeted by that ultraperfect Stepford wife of a secretary, Selena?" When Holden nodded and everyone else was paying attention, she continued, holding up the personnel files they'd taken from Tessara. "It seems Selena has a master's degree in biochemical science. Doesn't that seem a little bit of an overqualification for a secretary?"

Holden nodded slowly as Jane handed over the personnel file attached to Penny's. "Seems Penny personally recruited her from Stanford University two years ago. Why?"

"Good question," Jake said. "But if Penny had a hand in anything, it was usually for her own benefit. That woman was a sociopath. I don't trust anyone she would personally handpick as someone trustworthy."

"She gave me an odd vibe." Jane recalled the ultrachic woman with impeccable manners. "No one is that nice or perfectly put together."

"The question is, why is a highly trained scientist slumming it as a lowly gopher for a pharmaceutical company when she could've been in the lab?" Michelle mused. "Doesn't add up."

"Here's a thought...." Jane said. "Maybe it was a ruse to cover her tracks. No one is going to pay attention to a secretary. She's a ghost, moving in and out of people's offices without arousing suspicion. Honestly, it's the best cover, because everyone always overlooks the secretary."

Holden nodded. "And if Penny handpicked Selena, she had to have a reason. Let's dig into Selena's background and see what pops up." He grabbed Jake's computer and did a preliminary search but came up with nothing except benign Google entries. "Top of her class in Stanford, a member of Mensa and on the chess club."

Jake frowned. "What about family connections? Is there a possibility that Selena is related to Penny?"

"It doesn't say in her file," Jane answered, shaking her head. "But then it probably wouldn't if that was something they were trying to conceal. According to her file, Selena is twenty-six. I guess it's feasible for Selena to be Penny's daughter, but I would imagine something like that would eventually be known, right?"

"Penny used to serve in the military," Holden said. "That's how she met Tom and Ulysses. They served in the same unit. Do you think Penny had a kid overseas and left her behind when she returned stateside?"

"I shudder to think of that woman as a mother," Jake said grimly, then shook his head. "I don't know. Even if that theory is correct and Selena is related to Penny somehow and she's continuing her work…to what end?"

Jane shoved her hand through her hair, exasperated and exhausted. "I don't know," she admitted with a long exhale, and fell back against the sofa cushion. "Everything is starting to swim in my head. Maybe we're completely off base and spinning our wheels." She looked at Jake with sympathy. "How's Kat? She doing okay?"

"Yeah, she's just not accustomed to all this intrigue and danger. Does terrible things to her nerves. Can't blame her. This crap is getting old, even for me."

Holden nodded with a yawn. "You and me both, brother."

Michelle rubbed red-rimmed eyes and said, "I'm going to call it a night. I can't keep my eyes open any longer."

"Are you sure? Maybe you ought to stay here," Jake said, his voice hoarse from too much coffee and not enough sleep. "It's not safe at your place."

"Probably not, but I can't run out of fear. They've been controlling my life for too long and I'm done. Chances are my sister is already dead. You and I both know how this works. If they're going to try to take me out, they can do it on my turf, at the very least."

Jake nodded, though he didn't look happy about it. They all had military backgrounds and understood her need to stand her ground. "Keep your gun loaded and under your pillow."

"And sleep with one eye open," Holden tacked on. "With any luck we'll come out alive when this is all said and done."

"From your mouth to God's ear," Michelle said with a small smile before letting herself out.

"Kat's going to be upset that you let her go home," Holden said.

"Michelle has to do what she feels is right. I can only imagine the guilt and fear she's been living with," Jake said quietly. "You guys going to stay here tonight?"

"No, my place is pretty secure. Jane is staying with me." Jane, too tired to put up a fuss, merely nodded in agreement. That was Holden's cue to pack it in.

"We better call it a night, too. We'll contact you tomorrow if we find out anything more. What's Kat going to do?"

"I don't know. Call in sick, I imagine."

"Good idea. But watch your doors and windows. Bullets have been flying lately, if you know what I mean."

"I do." Jake accepted Holden's advice. "Keep your head down."

"Copy that." Holden collected Jane and they walked to the car, eyes trained in the darkness, ears on alert. Danger didn't always announce itself with a bang. Sometimes it sailed through on the wind.

Chapter 22

The following morning, Holden and Jane were gulping down fresh coffee after very little sleep and browsing the web when something on a news site snagged their attention. A woman's body had been found floating in the reflecting pool at the Lincoln Memorial.

Holden double-clicked the news report, and he swore under his breath. "The bastards killed her." Jane quickly scanned the short article.

"Michelle's sister?" Jane supposed, and Holden nodded. "The age seems right. If that's Michelle's sister, that means they're snipping loose threads right now. They must have what they've been after."

Seconds later, Holden's cell rang. It was Jake. "You see the news?" he asked.

"Yeah, just now. Was that Michelle's sister?"

"Yeah. She's devastated."

"Understandable. You know what this means…"

"Whatever plan they were setting in motion has begun," Jake answered. "And we still have nothing concrete to go on. We have no idea who's pulling the strings and no idea where to start."

"Not entirely true. We know something's up with Selena. I say we bring her in."

"We need more evidence," Jake disagreed. "If we pull the trigger prematurely, it'll end up blowing up in our faces."

"What, then?"

"Let's see what we can dig up on Selena first. Try to make those connections before we pull the alarm. You have anyone you can trust with this information?"

Holden thought of Chief Harris and nodded. "Yeah."

"Good. We're going to need all the backup we can muster. In the meantime, I'll start cultivating my own posse."

"Sounds good." They clicked off. Jane waited for Holden to share, which he did. "We're going to need James Cotton again."

She raised a brow. "To dig up dirt on Little Miss Perfect?"

"Yep."

"Sounds like a plan. What about Ulysses or Trevor?" she asked. "Maybe we ought to dig into their pasts, too."

"Couldn't hurt," Holden agreed, then, acting on impulse, he grabbed Jane and pulled her into a hard kiss. When they broke apart, they were both gasping for breath with pupils dilated.

"What was that for?"

"Because we're heading into some serious shit. I know at any moment either one of us could bite the big one, and I didn't want to take the risk of going into the hereafter without one last kiss from the most beautiful woman in the world."

Jane stared, her eyes welling with tears. "You're killing me," she said softly, her body melting against his. "And don't talk about dying. You're not going to die. And neither am I."

"Tomorrow is promised to no one," he reminded her gently without a hint of his usual smart-ass wise-cracking. He wanted to show her the raw side of what he was feeling, the stuff he couldn't quite put into words without fumbling like an idiot. "Jane, I know you have a lot of reasons why you and I don't work, but I can give you one reason why we do."

"Yeah?" The lilt of wary hope in her voice gave him courage. "What's that one reason?"

"This." He brushed his lips across hers in the sweetest, most tender kiss he'd ever given to another human being. In that single motion, he tried communicating that somehow she'd captured his heart in a way he didn't understand nor could truly verbalize, but he knew was true just as he knew the sun would rise every day. He was pretty damn sure he'd fallen in love with Jane Fallon and he wanted her to know, even if he couldn't say the words just yet.

She blinked back tears, and when she closed her eyes, moisture slid from the corners. "Why are you doing this?" she asked plaintively. "This isn't doing either of us any favors."

Disappointment crashed around him when she didn't seem to appreciate his grand gesture. He released her and tried not to let the bitterness of his letdown seep into his voice. "I just wanted to seize the moment," he said with a twist of his lips. "You know, in case."

She nodded but turned away from him, saying, "Well, let's focus on catching this SOB so we don't have to end up running for our lives, okay?"

Good plan. Following Jane's lead, he shoved his heartbreak under the proverbial rug and got on the horn with James Cotton.

Jane fought with her fluttering heart, hating that she was on the verge of a total meltdown after Holden's kiss. It'd felt like a goodbye kiss. As if he knew something she didn't, and she hated the very idea of Holden not being there across the conference table, giving her a hard time or trying to best her in the gym. She especially hated the idea of not being able to wake up each morning in his arms, but that was a separate problem she'd have to deal with later. Right now, they both needed their heads on straight if they were going to survive, which meant *stop freaking crying!* She surreptitiously wiped at her eyes and cleared her throat, determined to suck it up. They had very little time left on their clock, and no doubt the sniper was already loading his gun with bullets inscribed with their names. While Holden gave James instructions, she logged onto the computer and started looking for connections they might've missed last night. She cross-referenced Butterfly Bend winery to anyone else associated with Tessara aside from Penny Winslow, and when that came up empty, she started looking for ties to Selena and the cofounders of Tessara. The answer was there—she could feel it. And because it was so tantalizingly close, yet still just out of reach, she wanted to scream.

Within a few hours, James returned Holden's call. Holden put him on speaker so Jane could hear, too.

"You are not going to believe this, but…"

"Selena is Penny's daughter?" Holden answered. Jane half expected James to confirm, but when he didn't, her eyes widened in shock.

"Nope. I don't think pure evil can gestate," James quipped. "No, but she definitely has ties to Penny. Penny was her aunt."

"Aunt?" Holden repeated in surprise, mirroring Jane's expression. "How so?"

"Selena's the daughter of Trevor Granger. Trevor and Penny were half brother and sister, not cousins as they told everyone."

"You've got to be kidding me," Jane gasped. "How'd we miss that?"

"They weren't raised together and didn't let people

know they were actually siblings, preferring to tell everyone they were cousins."

"But why?"

"They were pretty close. Perhaps too close?" James guessed, grossing out both Holden and Jane.

"Are you saying…oh, God, that's disgusting," Holden said, grimacing. "So Selena is Trevor's daughter. Funny how he failed to mention his daughter worked at Tessara."

"Seems a little suspect on his part," Jane agreed. "But that alone is not a crime. We need more to go on."

"Well, today is your lucky day," James said with a cocky grin in his voice. "I have something you might find of use."

"Such as?" Holden asked.

"Selena's godmother is someone pretty important."

"Spit it out, Cotton," Holden said, losing patience. "We're in a bit of a time crunch."

"You take the fun out of everything. All right, all right, her godmother is none other than…the veep."

"The what?"

"You know, the veep…as in the vice president of the United States. Talk about connections."

Jane met Holden's astonished gaze, which she was sure matched her own. "Are you sure?" Jane asked before Holden could. "How did you find that out?"

"The internet is a wondrous place. It was fairly easy. Once I tracked down how Selena, Penny and Trevor connected, I just did background checks, verified birth records and whatnot and found the VP's name on the christening details kept at the church in the town where Selena was born. That's where I struck gold."

"You're a freaking genius." Holden grinned, but there was an edge of fear in his gaze and Jane knew where he was going with that. "So our connection to the higher power pulling the strings is the woman closest to the president."

"The one who stands to gain everything if something were to happen to the president," Jane finished. Holden nodded grimly. "Holy hell. We have to tell the chief."

"This is what Miko was trying to piece together," Holden said. "Thanks, James. You may have just saved the life of the president of the United States."

Holden and Jane barreled into Reed Harris's office but skidded to a stop when they saw who was having a conference with the chief.

"What's he doing here?" Jane asked in a low tone.

"Good question," Holden muttered. "The last time he was here, it was to poke around in our investigation. I doubt he's here to bring us a muffin basket."

"More's the pity. I'm starved," she quipped. "Let's welcome him to D.C., shall we?"

They walked into the chief's office and pinned Ulysses Rocha with twin looks of solid unwelcome. He had the grace to flush. "Morning, Chief," Holden said. "Mr. Rocha, Tessara must have some incredible frequent-flyer miles. To what do we owe this pleasure today?"

"I apologize for the way I handled myself the first time I came here. Unfortunately, I was operating under a different assumption, but I have information you might find of use to your investigation."

"Oh? Please share," Jane said with a smile that didn't reach her eyes.

"It's come to my attention that Selena may have misrepresented herself and misused company resources. I found this in an encrypted file." He handed a manila envelope to Holden. "Selena has been using Tessara to continue where Penny left off on many of her less-than-FDA-approved experiments. Mainly, Game Changer and Switchblade. As soon as I found out, I put a stop to it. We've only just recently begun to recover from the bad press Penny created, and I wasn't about to go another round with Selena."

"Where is she now?" Jane asked.

"I don't know," he admitted. "That's why I'm here. I'm sure with your resources you'll be able to find her a lot easier than I will. Of course, it goes without saying that when she finally surfaces, she's fired."

"She's more than fired...she's facing criminal and federal charges," Holden said. "Do you have any idea what she was planning?"

"Only that she was going to do something that would change the course of history. Naturally, I was concerned."

"Too bad you couldn't have been this concerned when we were first talking," Jane said with a wry twist of her lips. "A young woman might still be alive. Selena may have blood on her hands."

"Well, that's for you to work out. I've done my part," Ulysses said with a distasteful shudder. "I trust you can take it from here. I have a flight to catch."

Jane turned to the chief. "Are we just going to let him walk? Surely we've got him on obstruction, at the very least."

"We've got bigger problems. Let him go," Chief Harris said, waving them off and gesturing for the file. They closed the door behind Rocha as Reed said, "Let me take a look at what we've got here."

"Chief, we've got bigger problems indeed," Jane said. "We believe the vice president of the United States is plotting to use MCX-209 on the president and the executive branch at a special dinner slated for the end of this month."

"That's a very serious accusation," Chief Harris said, steepling his fingers. "You'd better know what you're talking about before you start saying that in mixed company."

"Selena's godmother is the VP. We think this plan has been in motion since way before Penny was killed and Selena just kept the plan in motion. We were sure there was something bigger at the top of the food chain pulling strings, and what bigger puppet master could there be than the VP?"

"And how would this be accomplished?" he asked.

"Through Selena's father's winery, Butterfly Bend. Tessara created a special coating for the cork that will be used to bottle the Presidential Reserve. My guess is they're planning to coat the cork with the MCX-209 so the wine is contaminated with the drug."

"Holy hell…" The chief looked green, but he snapped into action quickly. "If that's the case, we're in a heap of trouble, because that dinner is tonight."

"Are you sure?" Holden asked, frowning. "Trevor Granger told us it was at the end of the month."

"That was a security measure. The true date of the dinner is known only to a select few. We've got to get to that dinner and make sure no one drinks the wine."

Chapter 23

Teams flanked all exits of the executive dining room as the sounds of the dinner plating from the kitchen staff filled the air, along with the low hum of chatter. Michelle, Holden, Jane, Jake and Reed all headed up individual teams, covering all bases, while Kat waited for the all-clear. When the scene had been secured, the plan was for Kat to come in and verify if, in fact, MCX-209 was in play. Badges were flashed at the Secret Service, and they filed into the room to the surprised gasps of the dinner-party guests.

"Mr. President," Michelle said. "I apologize for the unorthodox appearance and for ruining your dinner, but we feel a threat to national security is in this room." She marched straight to the wine bottle directly in front of the president's plate.

The vice president, Gloria Burroughs, stood with an indignant expression, glowering at the intrusion. "What is the meaning of this? Explain yourself immediately," she demanded, looking to the Secret Service. "Remove these people. This is a private dinner and they are clearly misguided. There is no threat in this room. For heaven's sake, everyone in this room has been vetted."

The Secret Service shuffled, unsure of what to do. Michelle trained her gun on the vice president and the woman gasped, wilting against her chair. "Have you lost your mind? What are you doing?"

The president, a man with a shock of white hair and deep lines etched into his forehead, stared at Gloria with disappointment. He nodded to Michelle, who then brought Kat forward as Jake popped the cork on the wine, ran a swab over the bottom, then poured a droplet of a chemical solution on the swab. It turned green.

Kat announced, "This wine is contaminated with the experimental drug MCX-209. I would advise everyone to step away from the table so we can collect every bottle."

Gasps from around the room ensued, and Gloria paled as she stammered, "What is going on?"

"Don't bother to pretend innocence," Michelle said, as she put the VP in cuffs. "We've already informed the president of your connection to Butterfly Bend and your goddaughter, Selena. Gloria Burroughs, you are charged with treason against your country."

The president stood with a stern expression. "This breaks my heart, Gloria. I trusted you. How could you betray my trust like this? And what did you hope to gain?"

"Surely you can see I've been framed," Gloria said, clearly trying to appeal to the president's sense of fair play. "The evidence against me is purely circumstantial. I have many enemies—as do you. It wouldn't be a far stretch to frame me for this."

Michelle ignored the VP's protests and clicked the cuffs on the woman's wrists. "Where is Selena?" she asked, cinching the cuffs as tightly as they would go. Gloria winced, her eyes watered and her chin trembled. Hard to believe this was the mastermind. Right now she just looked like a scared old woman.

"Where is Selena?" she repeated.

Gloria, realizing the game was over, hung her head and whispered an address. Michelle handed the sobbing woman over to the Secret Service, and they hauled her away.

Michelle approached the president. "Thank you for taking a chance on our theory. We were pretty sure we had the answer, but there's always that one percent that can ruin everything."

"I'm so sorry to hear about your sister," he said, his voice kind. "Is there anything I can do for you? I'm in your debt. Your service and sacrifice to your country won't be forgotten."

Michelle blinked back tears. She hadn't had time yet to grieve—that would come later. She accepted the president's gratitude with stiff grace. "Thank you, sir. I haven't yet dealt with the pain of losing her, but I know it's there, waiting. I still can't believe she's gone."

"Anything you need, anything at all…don't hesitate," he told her, then turned to Holden and Jane, but most specifically to Holden. "Your brother was the one who first uncovered this plot?"

"Yes, sir."

"I owe him a great debt, as well. I understand he's no longer with us?"

"No, sir. He killed himself before he was able to uncover the true breadth and scope of the plot."

"I've seen his file. I don't care what the protocol is, I will not allow anyone to take his honor. He earned it and he will have it."

Holden blinked back tears. "Thank you, sir. That's all I ever wanted. Honor was everything to my brother."

"A good man. I'm sorry we lost him. If only he could've found his way to confiding in someone. It might've made the difference."

The president then turned to Chief Harris, his expression stern. "And what about Trevor Granger and his daughter, Selena?"

"A team will converge on the address Gloria gave us. Selena will be in custody soon," Chief Harris assured the president. "Right now, teams are processing the winery. Trevor Granger is cooperating fully. I doubt he had any knowledge of what his daughter was involved with. He seemed genuinely shocked at her duplicity."

"Our nation owes your team its gratitude."

Chief Harris accepted the praise with a stiff upper lip, but Michelle could tell he was grinning on the inside. Military men were all the same. So stoic.

Kat walked up to the president and said, "Sir, with your permission, I'd like to destroy MCX-209 for good. No more holding on to the formula or keeping a batch in the cooler. This is bound to happen again and again unless we completely destroy the drug and all traces of it."

The president nodded in understanding. "Seeing as I was almost a victim of this drug, I agree. It's too dangerous for anyone to have." He turned to Michelle. "Please see that this is done."

She inclined her head, and everyone in the room breathed more easily knowing MCX-209 was going to be nothing more than a bad memory from now on.

Jane and Holden, along with a team, converged on the property address Gloria had given up, but they found it empty.

"Damn it," Holden muttered under his breath after the property had been cleared. "She's a slippery one. Someone must've tipped her off."

Jane gestured for Holden, saying, "Come over here. I think we've got something."

As he joined her, Jane showed him a picture that floored him. It was of Miko and Selena. "Are you kidding me?" he asked, incredulous and feeling a little sick. "What the hell is this?"

"I think Miko and Selena were sleeping together,"

she said, biting her lip as she grimaced. "I mean, they look pretty cozy here."

Holden gripped the photo and stared at Miko holding Selena in his arms, grinning for the camera. Their body language told a story. A story that made Holden want to vomit.

"I don't understand," Holden said, looking to Jane for answers. "This doesn't make sense. Why was he with her?"

"Maybe she's the reason he killed himself. Maybe he found out he'd been sleeping with the enemy and had inadvertently given the wrong side valuable intel. For a man like your brother…I imagine that would be devastating."

"My brother wouldn't kill himself over a woman," he disagreed hotly, but something in that picture twisted in his gut. His brother was clearly enamored with the beautiful woman in his arms. Whether or not he'd known what she was capable of, Holden didn't know. He supposed he'd never know. Miko's secrets had died with him.

He crinkled the picture and let it drop from his fingers. "Let's go. Nothing's left for us here." Then he stalked from the house, needing some air.

"Holden, wait up," Jane called out after him, but he wasn't in the mood to chat. Everything he'd believed about his brother had been called into question because of that one picture. What about honor and integrity? It was easier for him to believe that Miko had died trying to do something honorable than the realization that he may have offed himself over a woman. No, he couldn't accept that. He just couldn't.

"Holden," Jane said. "We don't have the facts. Don't insert theories in the absence of facts, okay? For all we know, Miko had been using Selena to get information."

"He loved her." There was no sense in denying what he could see with his own eyes. "And he never once told me about her. I never knew. I was his twin brother. We never had secrets."

"But he wasn't a kid anymore. He was entitled to his own life, right?" she pointed out gently. "When I first started this investigation, I thought you were blinded by emotion in this case, but it turns out you were seeing clearly when the rest of us were blinded by prejudice. I saw a man who betrayed his country and I didn't care what his reasons were. You made me realize there was more to the story, and you helped save the president's life. Miko made mistakes because he was human, but I don't believe for a second he betrayed his country. Not for a second."

He met her gaze and saw truth reflecting back at him. Was he more upset that Miko had shut him out of his personal life or because his ego was bruised? Maybe it was best for him to leave Miko's personal life in the past. Maybe it was none of Holden's business.

"I'm so happy the president said what he did, because I'd planned to amend my report and request that Miko retain full honors in light of his contribution to our case. He doesn't deserve to be shamed. He gave his life, and that's the ultimate sacrifice."

Holden held back a wash of tears and jerked a nod. "Thank you," he managed to say before ducking out. He needed a moment.

A long moment.

Jane watched Holden go, and she thought about following. Something held her back, though. Holden was processing a lot about his brother, and she sensed he needed time to work it through.

The case was technically closed. A federal BOLO had been issued for Selena Weston, and it was only a matter of time before she was brought in. All that was left was to tie up loose ends and do the paperwork.

Which meant she no longer needed to stay with Holden. Time to go back to her place. She should be glad, but the knowledge filled her with sadness, as if she were losing something precious or leaving behind a loved one.

What had happened between them…it wasn't real, right? Extreme situations spiked temporary endorphins, simulating love and attraction. It would fade soon enough.

Right?

It hadn't the last time. Nothing about Holden seemed any less vivid in her heart than before. If anything, she was more conflicted than ever.

Just factor in the fact her father would never approve of Holden as a match and the ensuing World

War III that would follow, and that ought to put things in perspective.

But that empty feeling in the center of her chest remained, and no amount of logic and reason would dispel it. Holden was going to be a tough habit to break.

Jane withheld a deep sigh born of sadness and regret, but if there was one thing Fallons did well, it was soldier on.

So soldier on, girl.
Your heart will recover.
Eventually.

Chapter 24

Holden finished his second beer for the night, staring morosely at the gas flames from the fireplace as he picked at the paper encircling the bottle. So many questions and absolutely no chance of having them answered. Disgusted, he rose to get himself another beer when he stopped short. A woman melted from the shadows, a gun trained on his heart.

"Selena."

Ever the picture of perfection, the woman moved like a cat, soft on her feet and deadly focused. There was something sexy but frightening about her. Holden could see how Selena would've hooked Miko in a second.

"Archangelo boys...who knew they'd be the ruin of me."

A dark thrill chased through him, even though Selena had come to kill him. A slow, cold smile curved his lips.

"You're not going to win this. Your face is on every law enforcement agency's radar in every state, every town, every parish. Eventually, your luck will run out and they'll catch you."

"I know that."

"So why waste time with me?"

"Because I don't like loose ends."

And he was a loose end. "Is that what Miko was, too?"

A faint shadow passed over her features. "I loved him."

"I find that hard to believe."

Selena smiled coldly. "Is it hard to imagine he loved me, too?"

The idea made Holden ill. "I'm not much for fiction," he stated, watching her carefully. She'd come here for a reason, and it wasn't just to shoot him. "Why don't you stop playing around and tell me why you're here."

"You think I'm not here to kill you?"

"Not entirely."

"You're right. You have something I need."

His ears perked up. "Such as?"

"Miko had a thumb drive with sensitive information on it. I want it."

"And why would you need that?" he asked. "Want a little light reading while you're on the run?"

"I want to protect my father. Without that list, the

evidence against my father is circumstantial. Nothing is tying him to the wine. Penny was in charge of that deal. As far as the law is concerned, my father was an innocent victim, caught up in a deadly game he had no idea he was playing."

"But that's not the truth, is it? Your father knew exactly what was happening and was happy to cash in on the spoils."

She smiled. "Let's just say my father is a very smart man, but he'd never make it in prison. Too soft. And I'll do anything to protect him."

"What a good daughter. Too bad you take after Auntie Penny in the I-have-no-soul department."

Selena shrugged, then narrowed her gaze. "Where's the thumb drive?"

"Sorry, I can't give that to you. Guess you're going to have to shoot me, but you won't get it that way, either. It seems your plan is fundamentally flawed."

"Thanks for keeping it interesting," Selena said right before burying a bullet in his left leg.

He yelled and dropped to the floor.

"Now, about that thumb drive…" She walked to where he lay, pain spiking through his leg as blood poured from the wound, and smiled down at him, pointing the gun at his other leg. "Did you know you can riddle a body with bullets without actually killing a person? Hurts a lot, from what I hear. Auntie Penny was a very good teacher."

"You're not getting that drive," he gritted out. "You can fill me with holes and it won't matter. That list is going to save my brother's reputation. He was trying to take you down…only he didn't know it was you, did he?"

Selena walked to his kitchen and helped herself to a beer. "No, he didn't know at first. Miko…so damn noble. When he found out what Auntie Penny was having him do, it killed his sense of justice. It was actually hard to watch him self-destruct."

"Don't talk about my brother like you have the right."

"I have every right to talk about my lover. That's right, Holden…we were lovers. He was a beast in bed." She smiled coyly as she purred. "Is it true what they say about twins? That they're alike in all things? Are you a beast in bed, too?"

"Bitch, that's none of your business."

He and Selena whirled to find Jane, feet planted and gun pointed straight at Selena's chest. Without dropping her gaze from the woman, Jane said to Holden, "I can't leave you alone for two seconds and you have another woman up in your apartment. And to think I was coming to ask you to dinner."

"I've got her right where I want her," he groaned. "But feel free to take over. I'm a little busy bleeding out."

"Well, well, this is an exciting development. Jane Fallon, the agent with daddy issues. Come to play?"

"I wouldn't piss her off," Holden warned, blinking against the spots dancing before his eyes. Ah, crap… he was going to pass out from blood loss. Not very manly. "Could you hurry it up? I think I'm about to pass out."

"Tick tock," Selena murmured with a cold smile. "What are you going to do? Help him or shoot me? Can't do both."

The tiniest smile lifted the corner of Jane's mouth as she quipped, "Why not?" and she sent a bullet right through Selena's model-perfect shoulder, sending her crashing to the floor screaming. Selena struggled to rise to her feet, and Jane clocked her, knocking her out.

"Nice shooting, Tex." Holden winced as she helped him to the sofa. "Good God, this freaking hurts. Getting shot is no picnic."

"Surely this isn't your first bullet wound," she asked incredulously as she wound a kitchen towel around his leg and pulled it tight. "Afghanistan? Iraq? Chicago?"

"Sorry to disappoint you, but I tried to avoid getting shot," he answered, breaking out in a sweat. "So...you're saying you've taken a bullet?"

She laughed and pulled up her sleeve, showing off a small circular scar that punched in one side and went out the other. "A through and through in Uzbekistan. Hurt like a bitch, but I still managed to complete the mission and go out for drinks with my unit afterward."

He grinned as his vision dimmed. "You're such a badass, Jane Fallon. Will you freaking marry me?"

His vision began to smoke around the edges and he vaguely heard her answer as if shouted through a tunnel four miles long. "I just might have to in order to keep you out of trouble, Archangelo."

And then he blacked out completely, but he was pretty sure he was wearing a smile.

Jane couldn't believe how narrowly Holden had skated kissing the big one. The surgeon was able to patch him back up and, lo and behold, Jane matched his blood type and was able to donate to replace the blood he'd lost. The knowledge that her blood had played a part in saving him gave her warm tingles of happiness…well, that and putting a hole in that beautiful bitch, Selena. Yeah, that gave her really happy tingles.

Jane smoothed Holden's hair and watched him as he slept off the anesthesia. So much had changed in a very short amount of time. Her life would never be the same.

She'd lived her life trying to earn some modicum of respect from her father when, in fact, she didn't need anyone's approval. And that was exactly what she'd told her father. Once she'd realized she'd nearly lost the one man who'd never tried to make her feel less than the men around her, the one who thought she was damn awesome just the way she was, she'd found herself at her dad's house with a heart filled with purpose even if her hands were shaking.

"Dad, we need to talk," she'd said, moving past him when he'd started to bluster. "No, actually, you've done enough talking in your life—you're going to listen while I do the talking."

"What's come over you?" he'd asked gruffly.

"Reality, Dad. That's what's come over me. I'm

tired of paying for the sins of my mother. I'm my own person and I'm a pretty great person. Here's the thing, Dad…I've spent my life trying to earn a smidge of your approval and I've never really gotten it because all this time you've been punishing me for being a girl. Or maybe you're punishing me because I look so much like my mother. I don't know and I don't care. It's over. I just helped uncover a plot to wipe out the president and half of his executive board. That's right—me. The one you think can't wipe her ass without assistance."

"Watch your mouth. I didn't raise you to be disrespectful," he'd said sharply, but she wasn't about to be cowed into silence. Not this time.

"See, there you go again. You can't even give me a single word of praise after I just told you that I saved the freaking president of the United States. And you know what? I don't need your approval any longer. I love you, I really do, but I'm sick and tired of your bullshit. And another thing—it's time you either hire an accountant or do your checkbook yourself because I have a life to plan."

She had left him sputtering in his chair, and she didn't feel the least bit guilty. In fact, the smile curving her lips felt just about perfect.

Holden had helped her realize that it was more important to live by your own code than try to conform to someone else's. She wished she'd known Miko the man so she could see him as Holden did; she had a feeling she would've liked him.

She wasn't entirely sure if Holden had meant

what he said when he'd asked her to marry him, but she knew she was ready to take a chance at a relationship—a real relationship where they watched movies at night, had sleepy morning sex and stashed a toothbrush at each other's places. Yeah, the real deal, not partners with benefits. A smile found her. She liked the sound of that. No, actually…she loved the sound of that.

But you know what? She loved the sound of something else too…Jane Archangelo. It had a nice ring to it.

She leaned in and nuzzled Holden's neck, inhaling his scent and committing it to memory. Whispering against the shell of his ear, she said, "I don't know how you did it, but somewhere along the way, you made me fall in love with you. What do you think about that?"

Holden sighed softly in his sleep, and she brushed a kiss across his mouth. "I'll take that as confirmation that you are tickled pink." She grinned. "Now, hurry up and get better. I think we have a wedding to plan."

Epilogue

Holden and Jane stood at attention as Miko Archangelo was given the military funeral he deserved with full honors intact. The white-gloved marine officer presented Holden with the American flag, saying in a tone steeped in respect, "On behalf of the president of the United States, the United States Marine Corps and a grateful nation, please accept this flag as a symbol of our appreciation for your loved one's honorable and faithful service."

Blinking back tears, Holden accepted the flag and held it tightly. *This is for you, brother.* A life without his twin flashed before his eyes, and it was almost more than he could stand. True grief rolled over him for the first time since hearing the news that Miko was dead. But even as the grief hurt, the pain was cathartic. He could finally let Miko go. His brother's integrity had been salvaged and they'd managed to finish the work Miko had failed to complete. Selena Weston was rotting in federal prison along with her father, Trevor Granger, and Holden had the most beautiful woman in the world at his side. All in all, things couldn't have ended better. Oh, and as a happy side note, MCX-209 would never see light again. Every shred of documentation and sample had been incinerated, so at the very least anyone suffering from memory loss would do so by natural causes.

"You good?" Jane asked, looking to him with love in her eyes.

"I'm golden." He sniffed back manly tears. "It's a good day." And he meant it. A hawk screeched overhead and he chuckled.

Miko, wherever you are, I hope you're kicking back enjoying a cold one, buddy. You earned it.

* * * * *

ROMANTIC suspense

Available November 4, 2014

REQUEST YOUR FREE BOOKS!
2 FREE NOVELS PLUS 2 FREE GIFTS!

🅷 HARLEQUIN®

ROMANTIC suspense

Sparked by danger, fueled by passion

YES! Please send me 2 FREE Harlequin® Romantic Suspense novels and my 2 FREE gifts (gifts are worth about $10). After receiving them, if I don't wish to receive any more books, I can return the shipping statement marked "cancel." If I don't cancel, I will receive 4 brand-new novels every month and be billed just $4.74 per book in the U.S. or $5.24 per book in Canada. That's a savings of at least 14% off the cover price! It's quite a bargain! Shipping and handling is just 50¢ per book in the U.S. and 75¢ per book in Canada.* I understand that accepting the 2 free books and gifts places me under no obligation to buy anything. I can always return a shipment and cancel at any time. Even if I never buy another book, the two free books and gifts are mine to keep forever.

240/340 HDN F45N

Name	(PLEASE PRINT)	
Address		Apt. #
City	State/Prov.	Zip/Postal Code

Signature (if under 18, a parent or guardian must sign)

Mail to the **Harlequin® Reader Service:**
IN U.S.A.: P.O. Box 1867, Buffalo, NY 14240-1867
IN CANADA: P.O. Box 609, Fort Erie, Ontario L2A 5X3

Want to try two free books from another line?
Call 1-800-873-8635 or visit www.ReaderService.com.

* Terms and prices subject to change without notice. Prices do not include applicable taxes. Sales tax applicable in N.Y. Canadian residents will be charged applicable taxes. Offer not valid in Quebec. This offer is limited to one order per household. Not valid for current subscribers to Harlequin Romantic Suspense books. All orders subject to credit approval. Credit or debit balances in a customer's account(s) may be offset by any other outstanding balance owed by or to the customer. Please allow 4 to 6 weeks for delivery. Offer available while quantities last.

Your Privacy—The Harlequin® Reader Service is committed to protecting your privacy. Our Privacy Policy is available online at www.ReaderService.com or upon request from the Harlequin Reader Service.

We make a portion of our mailing list available to reputable third parties that offer products we believe may interest you. If you prefer that we not exchange your name with third parties, or if you wish to clarify or modify your communication preferences, please visit us at www.ReaderService.com/consumerschoice or write to us at Harlequin Reader Service Preference Service, P.O. Box 9062, Buffalo, NY 14269. Include your complete name and address.

HRS13R

Pink panties.

Hot pink panties.

Flint closed the door to his master bedroom and began to
change out of his uniform.

He'd gone into the store on high alert, hovering near
Nina and watching to make sure that nobody else got close
to her.

What he hadn't realized was that shopping with a woman
could be such an intimate experience. He'd been fine as
she'd grabbed several T-shirts and sweatshirts, some jogging
pants and a nightshirt.

His close presence next to her felt a little more intrusive as
she shopped for toiletries. Peach-scented shampoo joined a
bottle of peach and vanilla scented body cream. It was then
that things began to get a little wonky in his head.

He imagined her slathering that lotion up and down her

shapely legs and rubbing it over her slender shoulders. He imagined the two of them showering together, the scent of peaches filling the steamy air as he washed the length of her glorious hair and then stroked a sponge all over her body.

He'd finally managed to snap himself back into professional mode when she'd headed to the intimates section. He was okay when she grabbed a white bra and threw it into the shopping basket. He even remained calm and cool when the bra was followed by a package of underpants.

It was when she tossed that single pair of hot pink panties in the cart that his head once again went a little wonky. Pink panties and peach lotion, those things had been all he'd been able to think about.

He sat on the edge of his bed to get every inappropriate vision and thought he'd had of Nina over the past couple of hours out of his head.

She was the witness to a vicious crime and a victim of arson. She was here to be in his protective custody, not to be an object of his sexual fantasies. Speaking of protective custody, he pulled himself off the bed, grabbed his gun and went in search of his houseguest.

**Don't miss
HER COLTON LAWMAN
by *New York Times* bestselling author
Carla Cassidy, coming November 2014 from**

⊕HARLEQUIN®

ROMANTIC suspense

HRSEXP1014

HARLEQUIN®

ROMANTIC suspense

Heart-racing romance, high-stakes suspense!

TEXAS STAKEOUT
by *New York Times* bestselling author
Virna DePaul

A killer in waiting. A brother in hiding.
Could they be the same person?

Dylan Rooney is out of his element. A U.S. marshal and
city-wrangler at heart, he must adopt a new cover—and a
new client—in the heart of Texas. The assignment: protect
Rachel Kincaid...a widow with a young son who realizes her
struggles are just beginning when her ranch hand is killed.
Posing as the new ranch hand, Dylan quickly learns that
catching a killer may not be so simple—especially when
Rachel's fugitive brother is the prime suspect. And the
woman he's vowed to protect is the same woman he's
falling in love with.

Available **NOVEMBER 2014**
Wherever books and ebooks are sold.

www.Harlequin.com

HRS78954

ROMANTIC suspense

Heart-racing romance, high-stakes suspense!

HIGH-STAKES BACHELOR
by Cindy Dees

*More than hearts are at stake for a legendary Hollywood family in Cindy Dees' brand new miniseries, **The Prescott Bachelors!***

Wannabe stuntwoman Ana Izzolo can't believe she lands a starring role in actor-producer Jackson Prescott's new film. A plain-Jane nobody and a megastar? Their on-screen chemistry is electric, burning up the celluloid...but offscreen, Ana is stalked by danger.

Like a true Hollywood hero, Jackson whisks her to his oceanfront mansion, practicing love scenes while keeping her safe. But when their real-life relationship starts mirroring the movie's leading couple, the confirmed bachelor fears he may fall for the doe-eyed ingenue. If the stalker doesn't get her first....

Available **NOVEMBER 2014**

Wherever books and ebooks are sold

www.Harlequin.com

HRS78947

HARLEQUIN®

ROMANTIC suspense

Heart-racing romance, high-stakes suspense!

DESIGNATED TARGET
by **Karen Anders**

A NCIS agent must protect a brainy scientist who criminals are after—for her mind.

NCIS special agent Vincent Fitzgerald's mission: to find missing naval scientist Dr. Skylar Baang. The brilliant American-Filipino beauty has been kidnapped for her brain and research on top secret projects. But even as Vin rescues her from a dangerous group, he knows they'll be back.

A long-ago promise has kept Skylar committed to her work—love is a distraction she's never allowed herself. Now in the protective custody of a complicated NCIS agent who surprises her at every turn, Skylar wants to stop thinking and start *feeling*. But as the thugs come after her, she'll need everything she is—and smart, sexy Vin—to stay alive.

Available **NOVEMBER 2014**
Wherever books and ebooks are sold.

HRS78961

HARLEQUIN®
A *Romance* FOR EVERY MOOD™

Love the Harlequin book you just read?

Your opinion matters.

Review this book on your favorite book site, review site, blog or your own social media properties and share your opinion with other readers!

Be sure to connect with us at:
Harlequin.com/Newsletters
Facebook.com/HarlequinBooks
Twitter.com/HarlequinBooks